Al Normann

HUNTING HUMANITY

AL NORMANN

Hunting Humanity
Copyright © 2023 by Al Normann

This is a work of fiction any resemblance to any person living or dead is coincidental

Editor Jasmine Redford

Tellwell Talent
www.tellwell.ca

ISBN
978-0-2288-9281-6 (Hardcover)
978-0-2288-9280-9 (Paperback)
978-0-2288-9282-3 (eBook)

DEDICATION

This book is dedicated to Stephen whose
patient encouragement was instrumental
in me actually writing it down

ONE

———————

Daganu woke up to the morning chill. He reached for the sleeping fur but it was gone. Rousing himself slightly he saw that the others sleeping under the fur had rolled away from him. These things happened when you were the one sleeping at the edge of the group. He briefly considered reclaiming his portion of the fur but the darkness of night was fading into morning grey. He might as well get up instead.

Rising, he put on his day furs and tied on his smoked hide belt. Exiting the hut he looked at the sky. The light was strong enough that he could see scattered wispy clouds. They neither looked nor smelled of rain. It would be a pleasant day.

He stepped to his left to urinate. There was a shrub that he had watered every morning since the Kakass had come to this camp. Gentle steam rose from the spot. After finishing he walked to the fire for its radiant comfort.

The only person there was Bathen, the keeper of the night fire. Daganu was a lone hunter and as such knew all the basic magic associated with the building and care of fires, but Bathen knew it all. The keeper of the night

1

fire was the most important person in the clan. Bathen even outranked even the chief. Every night it was his duty to tend the fire and protect the clan from demons and animals, which everyone knew were most active at night. This responsibility was too important to leave to someone else.

Bathen had students. The most advanced of them would one day become the keeper of the night fire when Bathen could no longer perform all of the night duties, but until then the senior student would be the keeper of the day fire. Between the two of them Bathen and his senior student protected the clan from sun to sun. Angry demons and spirits were largely held at bay and few animals bothered the camp while they knew there was someone awake and alert. Of course, all the hunters must respond if an alarm was raised, but this rarely happened.

Daganu squatted on his haunches by the fire on the opposite side from Bathen. Bathen looked at Daganu but said nothing. Bathen rarely spoke unless he had something to say. The quiet suited Daganu well, as he was comfortable with silence, which was almost a prerequisite for being a lone hunter.

Lone hunters were not common among the Kakass. Most men needed a certain amount of companionship to be comfortable. Daganu was an exception. When he set out on the hunt everybody knew he would probably be gone until he had killed something substantial. From time to time the clan would have moved campsites before his return but this was rarely a problem. Unless there was an enemy to be avoided the clan left an easy trail to follow.

The two of them crouched comfortably by the fire. There wasn't much flame. There was no need. It was late in the spring, almost summer, and it was not cold, so having heat was not an issue, nor were there predators or scavengers about. A bright fire might attract hostile members of other clans. However, inter-clan fighting had not happened in recent years, so an attack was unlikely. Still, it was best to be cautious.

Inexperienced fire tenders often got flare-ups when they added more fuel to the fire. This rarely happened when Bathen cared for a fire. He was an artist. His fires hovered on the edge of flaring. If sudden light was needed it could be achieved in the space of a few long breaths.

As they sat quietly together Daganu scratched himself. His fingers found a small, hard body. Carefully, he pulled the flea away from his body. With satisfaction he flipped it into the centre of the heat. The flea sizzled briefly.

Daylight came softly. The stars faded away as the sky turned blue. The textures of the view changed as the light now invaded. The soft and mysterious night transformed into the sharpness and clarity of day. The sunward horizon caught fire as Ohlah, the sun, approached carrying the day. The view of the mountain top behind the men became bright and vibrant.

Bathen stood, eyes fixed upon the brightest spot on the sunward horizon. The brightness which had begun upon the peak flowed down the slope to the camp. When the light reached Bathen he spread his arms, closed his eyes and briefly basked in the comforting heat of the morning sunshine.

"Great Sun Ohlah welcome.

"Great Sun Ohlah we thank you for your gift of day."

Night had ended.

His responsibility fulfilled, Bathen sat once more beside the fire. He and Daganu quietly kept one another company as the camp came to life around them.

They began to hear people stirring and quietly speaking in the huts. Kakass huts were built of thatching over a skeleton of branches. The materials for each hut were always whatever was in abundance in the area they happened to be in. In this case the frameworks were made from small dead spruce which had died in a recent forest fire. The thatching consisted of lush green spruce branch ends from an unburned area on the other side of the clearing.

Always an early riser, Huth was the first to emerge. Huth was the oldest member of the clan. He remembered the chief as a little girl, and occasionally embarrassed her with his stories of the mischief she had made.

Huth had been a mighty hunter in his day. When the hunters cornered dangerous game he was always in the forefront. He was a tireless hunter and his spear was most often the weapon that brought the animal down.

He had also been the best of the flint knappers. To have a spear made by Huth was to have the best. His hand axes, knives and hide working blades were possessions to be proud of. Those times were long past. Huth's strength had faded and his hair was white. Sometimes an elder of the clan suffered from stiffening and painful joints, and this had happened to Huth. His knuckles and finger joints were swollen; gripping objects tightly caused him agony. He might have ignored the pain and gone hunting anyway, but his eyes had turned cloudy and he could no longer see much more than light and dark.

When the clan moved the camp from one place to another, Huth had difficulty travelling at the pace of the main group. One of the younger hunters would walk with him at a pace set by the old man. They often arrived at the new encampment long after the main body of the clan.

However, accompanying Huth was considered to be a great honour.

It was a rare day when no hunter came to him for advice. His many years had gifted him with deep knowledge and wisdom. In spite of all his problems, Huth was seldom in a sour mood. If no advice was needed, he could often be coaxed to tell stories. The way he told a story was more entertaining than any other clan member's. This was one of the reasons he was seldom alone.

As the middle of the day neared, Daganu began collecting his hunting gear. The camp still contained meat, but the supply was running low. The main group of hunters were discussing what animals could be found, and where, but from long experience Daganu knew they were unlikely to set out for a day or two. This delay had always annoyed him. While the others liked to have a clear goal in mind before beginning anything, Daganu's attitude had always been Just Do It. Just Do It was the reason he had first gone hunting by himself.

His first solo hunt had been a revelation. He learned that he truly enjoyed the solitude. He also discovered a talent for nearly silent movement and that, if he was alone, he could get remarkably close to his prey. His philosophy of Just Do It did not arise from a lack of patience. Indeed, he was more willing than any of the other hunters to spend large periods of time in the stalk. If he thought that an animal was nearby on a silent day, he would remain motionless for long periods of time while waiting for some natural noise that could mask his movements. Birds were especially good sound cover.

Daganu really liked birds.

This style of hunting had an additional benefit. He had discovered that while hunting in this manner he was fully focussed, and by using every sense he had it made him feel more intensely alive than at any other time. Also, the feeling of satisfaction after a successful hunt was even deeper than what he felt as part of a group. This was not to say that collective hunts were not a pleasure; they had the added benefit of a strong companionship, and to sharing success was satisfying. It was simply that, for Daganu, solo hunting was … better.

He was in no hurry. By the time he arrived at his destination it would not be the best time of day to hunt. He checked the pouches on his belt to be certain that he was not forgetting something. He had his fire drill and tinder. He also had a stone hand axe, a plentiful supply of cord which he had braided from strong green grass, a small supply of medicinal herbs and some fragrant grasses for ceremonial purposes.

He carried two spears. One was a light, carefully balanced throwing spear. The other was a sturdier spear meant for close quarter handheld work. Both spears had heads made of stone. These most important tools of the hunter were inspected to be certain the points were solidly attached and the shafts had not somehow been damaged;

it was vitally important that a spear not break in use. He also had an empty water bladder to carry along. In this area streams were abundant but this was not true of every place. However, water was heavy and so there was no good reason to fill the bladder when he would never be far from a source of water to drink. If he was heading into an area he was not familiar with then he would fill the bladder.

Everything passed inspection.

Much of his gear he had made himself, but the spear points were an exception. The stone they were made from could not be found on their territory but could only be sourced from a wandering trader. It was so important that the spears function perfectly that the clan's stone points were made almost entirely by whatever clansman had the greatest skill in stone knapping.

His knife he had made himself. The flint blade was fixed onto a spruce handle with sinew and pine pitch. It was very sharp. Daganu smiled to himself as he remembered the first time he had tried flint knapping. The scar on his left hand was still clearly visible and probably would be for the rest of his life.

Daganu checked his digging stick. It was a woman's tool, but only a fool ignores dependable food when on a trek. Besides, when you are alone you must do every task. All hunters must learn some things, such as basic fire magic. Beyond learning how to build and feed a fire Daganu had gone to Bathen and acquired the basic incantations. What is the point of a fire on a warm night beyond cooking? It is the conduit to communication with the gods.

This training did not make Daganu Bathen's apprentice; Bathen already had apprentices, and the best of them was the keeper of the day fire, Akel. Yet without god appeasing magic any person away from the clan fires was needlessly vulnerable.

Daganu had also gone to Simfa, chief of the clan and eldest among the women. From her he learned more of herb lore. All hunters learn something of plant wisdom. They must be able to find reliable and edible plants. To this basic knowledge Daganu added some standard healing magic. Of course, some plant magic was forbidden to men. All know that women need moon magic, but it was understood that there is some extra magic to deal with child bearing, nursing and probably other things hidden from men. Daganu had no interest in that; he already had enough to deal with.

With the packing complete, the young hunter sat back until the timing felt right. This camp sat in a relatively level part of a mountain meadow. Such level areas were not found on the majority of mountainside meadows, so the good sites were used over and over. As usual the camp had been situated near a small stream that flowed nearby. Not far off was a suitable stand of trees with a selection of fallen and standing dead wood; a fire gets hungry and it must be fed.

Everything was ready. He sat back to watch the activity of the camp. There was only one baby in the camp; all the other children were at least toddlers. The baby began to cry. Her mother picked the infant up and began to nurse her.

Daganu barely remembered his own mother. She had died of a fever when he was very young. His father had died on a hunting trip before he was born. He had been moving silently to sneak up on a sheep. His father, he was told, was very good at moving silently. The mistake he made was to focus exclusively on his prey. He did not see the mother bear or her cubs until he was between them, and by then it was too late. The mother bear mauled him severely because she thought he was a threat to her cubs. The other hunters carried him back but he did not live long enough to reach the camp.

After his mother died Daganu grew up cared for by the entire clan. While it is best to have one's parents doing the daily parenting, he had never lacked for food, clothing or affection.

He enjoyed the laughter of the small children as they ran squealing through the camp. Daganu remembered playing those games not so long ago. There is a certain wistful feeling attached to such memories. It is good to be grown and a provider for your people, but in childhood there is a freedom never to be found again. Days are for playing, and when you become hungry you go to the fire to see what food is to be had. There is usually something to eat. The Kakass seldom went hungry.

Meat was the first choice among foods, but the bulk of the diet tended to be plants which were gathered by the women. The wanderings of the clan were largely determined by what plants were in season. The women held the clan's knowledge of such things and so it was usually they who decided when it was time to move, and to where. Naturally there were exceptions. Times of animal migration overruled all else. Some animals moved in such large herds that no area could feed them for long. So, like the Kakass, they wandered, and like the Kakass such wanderings were predictable. Success in hunting these animals depended upon the clan reaching the grazing grounds slightly ahead of the animals.

Fish also could migrate. Spawning runs in the rivers were bonanzas not to be missed.

Birds migrated too, but they were normally out of reach. There were places where some techniques could be used for the successful hunting of birds, but the Kakass did not live in such an area. They mostly left bird hunting to other clans.

The abundant food was not wasted. Meat and fish were smoked and dried so that it could be stored for a considerable time. This work was one of the first tasks children assisted the adults with, and it was eagerly anticipated by the children. It was an early step in becoming a grown up.

However, there was no spawning run or land animal migration due for quite some time. At these times the authority to govern the clan's movement rested with the women, and they were content with their current location. The roots and greens of the season were far from being depleted here, and life was good.

By the stream were some of the women. They had just bathed and were now busy braiding each other's hair. The air was alive with the sounds of women chattering and happy children playing. Things were as they should be.

Daganu now felt it was time to leave. Several of the clan called a farewell as he walked through the camp, and Daganu gestured acknowledgement. He was already in hunting mode and so did not speak. He was a man of few words in any case.

Late afternoon found Daganu travelling through a pass and on the other side of the mountain. While still in the pass he had spotted a marmot sunning itself. It was well within his spear casting range. The marmot now rode hanging from his belt as if it were another one of his tools. Daganu glanced at it from time to time, and it made his appetite grow.

A clear and tumbling brook crossed his path. It was a good time of day to make a camp so he turned to follow it down the slope. Soon he was in a luxuriant growth of spruce.

Not far to the side he spotted a windfall spruce tree with its roots pulled out of the ground and still clutching a sizeable burden of soil. The soil that had been clutched by the roots left behind a shallow pit. As it sometimes happens, as the tree fell the roots on the downwind side did not break and the base of the trunk remained held well above the mossy ground. It was an excellent find.

He untied his belt and dropped it beside the pit the roots had excavated. He then shrugged off his day furs and laid them beside the pit as well. Upon the furs he placed his fire drill, a tinder fungus, some dry, dead grass, his empty water bladder, and his hand axe.

The next step was to collect firewood. Fire is a fussy eater when it is young, so the first trip out was for collecting very thin dry twigs. Larger wood is needed once the fire is born. Left to itself a fire will greedily gobble more and more small materials, faster and faster, with no actual limit Like a small child it must be guided to a more suitable diet, so larger branches are introduced, building in stages up to full sized limbs, and these, too, must be collected.

If you know what you are doing and a good source is nearby, the preparations really don't take very long.

Fire fodder collected, Daganu picked up his axe and settled himself beneath the trunk of the fallen spruce. He chopped away those branches which were pointing down into the space beneath it. After he had enough room to comfortably lie beneath the trunk, these branches were carried out and then set into the outside branches to make a wind and water barrier, important if an early summer storm should blow in. The few branches from beneath the trunk were not enough to finish his barrier, so Daganu collected low lying branches from nearby to fill the gaps to his satisfaction. He left his axe back on his furs because if a branch was large enough to need an axe for collecting, it was too coarse for the task in any case. These branch tips were collected simply by tearing them from the trees by hand.

There was still good daylight when he had completed his work and was satisfied with his camp. If he knew that he would be leaving on the following day he would not have bothered to build such a complex shelter, but in this case he was not certain how long he might linger in the area. He might find enough big game animals close by to warrant a prolonged stay.

Daganu was something of a specialist. He would never ignore a chance to take sheep, goats, deer and the like, but his focus was forever the great deer. These creatures stood man high and the males, in season, carried enormous antlers. The meat of just one would feed the clan for a long time, and antler was the best material for making tools. It was second only to high quality stone.

Whenever he brought down a great deer Daganu would gut it, make a full pack of meat and go directly back to the clan camp. There would be far more meat than he could transport by himself; he would need help. He would lead a group to the kill site and together they would carry the meat home.

That is what would happen unless it was nearing the time to move the camp. Then the simplest solution would be to move the camp itself to the kill.

Fantasizing about great successes that may lie in the future is a pleasant diversion, but there is always something to be done in the present.

Using his fire drill and the materials he had gathered Daganu prepared to start a fire inside the excavation created when the spruce fell. Such a hole exposes the mineral soil, and that makes a safe place to hold the fire. Fire was vital, but if the fire maker was careless it could escape and try to eat the entire forest.

After preparing a sort of nest made of dry grass and small twigs, he took a small piece of the tinder fungus he carried. Laying it on the ground he placed his base board, made of dry willow, beside it. This board had one flat side on which he had carved a shallow hole with a notch on one edge. His spindle was a piece of straight cedar which was sharpened to the right size to fit into the hole. He began to spin his drill with the ease of long practice. It did not take long for him to produce smoke and a glowing coal which he carefully transferred onto his tinder. Steady blowing soon produced a flame which he moved to his grass and twig nest.

Fire had been made.

Some clan members wondered about the righteousness of letting the fire die. Bathen told them that fires had a short life and that if all was done with respect no offense would be taken.

He had left a larger space between the fire and the soil filled root crown than he normally would. This arrangement allowed him to roast the marmot between the two, taking advantage of the heat reflected from the uplifted soil. First, of course, he took from one of his pouches some flavouring herbs and rubbed them onto the meat.

He thought to himself, "I do run a civilized camp."

Marmot is tasty and has a good layer of fat. The juices bubbled and ran down the sides to drip onto the ground. He had nothing to catch the drippings with. You can't carry everything with you.

When you make a kill it is proper to ask the blessing of the god of the hunt. Daganu took the tail and the four paws of the marmot and reverently placed them into the fire.

"Atta accept this offering," he intoned. "Atta bless this hunt."

He watched as his offerings slowly burned away. You do not eat until the god has finished. That would be very bad manners. Eventually the tail and paws were gone. The flames had taken them away to wherever it is that flames go.

Daganu ate slowly, enjoying the tender meat. There is a special pleasure in dining on the fruits of your hunt. He broke the long bones and sucked out the marrow. There is not much marrow on a marmot, but it is delicious.

The bones were placed on the marmot's hide which was then rolled up. This he set aside. For a while he sat by his fire watching the flames.

Eventually he took his furs and belongings into his shelter and went to sleep.

Daganu awoke in terror.

The very ground itself was moving beneath him. He struggled to rise but could not manage to gain his balance. The ground shook for what seemed like forever.

He had no concept of what an earthquake was. Simfa was the teller of tales for the clan. She taught the knowledge of the Kakass, mostly around the night fire when all the clan were gathered together. Included in the stories were teachings of the gods, how the clan members were expected to behave and why and explanations of the world itself Nowhere in her collection of stories could you find any mention of an earthquake. They were simply too rare in their part of the world to be bothered with.

The shaking stopped.

Daganu lay wide eyed and still in the night.

Then from the direction of the Kakass encampment came a roar unlike any he had heard before. The depth of it and the volume of the sound far exceeded even that of the sabretooth, the giant longtoothed cat. The sound briefly froze Daganu into immobility.

He then burst into activity. He scrambled around the trunk of the fallen spruce to the ashes of his fire where the coals were still glowing. Grabbing fire starting twigs he blew upon them and swiftly rebuilt it into flame. To this revived flame he added larger pieces and soon had that rarest of fires for his people, that of a roaring bonfire.

Into this he thrust the skin wrapped remnants of the marmot.

"Atta shield me," he quavered, claiming the hunting god as his personal protector. "Atta protect me. Ohlah shield me. Ohlah protect me." The sun god was always a good choice to pray to because Ohlah watched everything that happened during the day. Ohlah's wisdom was great.

The roaring had trailed off into a deep silence.

"Atta shield me. Atta protect me. Ohlah shield me. Ohlah protect me."

He continued his mantra until he could find no trace of the marmot remains. Then, wide eyed and terrified, he lay silent by the dubious comfort of the fire until dawn.

That was the longest night in Daganu's life.

He ceased to feed the fire when the light grew to the point that he could see clearly, but he did not rise until Ohlah the sun had fully arisen. He had invoked the protection of the sun god as well as the hunting god, so he wanted Ohlah to be completely awake before doing anything that might attract attention. Then he gathered his gear. He checked to be sure the fire was out before leaving. Some things are too deeply ingrained to be neglected.

He set out to return to his clan. When faced with an unprecedented dilemma you need to consult with a more knowledgeable authority. He must speak with Bathen. He made the trip back far faster than yesterday's trip out.

If felt far longer.

Eventually he reached what he knew to be the last rise on the mountain's shoulder before he could sight the camp. He was following a game trail. The camp area had been chosen in large part for the abundance of game in the vicinity. His eyes were on this trail because there were fresh tracks heading away from the camp. Clearly the sheep that had made the tracks were panicked because he had never seen so much fresh dirt kicked up before. The animals were clearly fleeing from whatever monster had made the terrible sound from last night.

Then he looked up and froze.

The camp was not where it should be. The very meadow it had been in was gone as was the slope it had been on. A portion of the mountain was missing. An enormous scar of tumbled boulders ran all the way down the slope to the bottom of the valley, or rather to where the bottom of the valley had been. The valley floor had been partially filled. The rubble extended all the way across the valley and part of the way up the slope of the mountain on the far side.

Daganu found himself on his knees. He had no memory of how that had happened. Motionless he stared uncomprehendingly at the place where everybody he knew should be.

Oh gods.

Oh gods.

Oh gods.

No.

TWO

It was before midday when Daganu had first sighted the scar of the landslide. The shock of it had brought him to his knees. It was now well into the afternoon if the position of the sun was to be believed. What had happened to the time in between Daganu had no idea. All he knew was that he was still in the same spot and that his legs were in agony from the lack of circulation. It was this pain that had brought him out of his funk.

He could not make his legs obey his wishes. He pitched forward and lay prone while the blood flow re-established itself. It hurt. He almost welcomed the distraction. As he lay there he became aware of a raging thirst. It occurred to him that he had not had so much as a sip of water all day. As for appetite, he had none.

It was obvious that the stream that had run past the camp no longer existed. When he could stand up on legs that still felt wooden he began to retrace his steps. Small streams were abundant in that place and season. He made his way to the nearest and drank deeply. He then sat upon a convenient boulder and gazed numbly at the flowing water.

Eventually he looked around. It was apparent that the shadows had moved again. More time must have elapsed.

Rising, he began to move. He knew not where he was going. He was operating purely on reflex. After a while he realized he was standing in front of his previous night's shelter. He gazed at it blankly. After a time he crawled into it, wrapped his furs around him, and laid down.

The sun had not set but that was irrelevant. He was not sleeping. He was not much of anything. He was barely even alive.

Night came.

Morning, when it replaced night, was foggy and cool. Daganu was beginning to be self-aware again.

He needed to return to the site of the slide. It was possible that someone of the clan had been out of the camp and so had survived. He knew that such a thing was unlikely, but he ignored that thought; desperate people cling to shreds of hope.

He travelled again to the dreaded site and he spent the day walking the periphery of the slide looking for traces of some other survivor.

There were none.

Sunset found him once more at his windfall spruce shelter. He built another fire. As he gazed into the flames, he remembered sounds and scenes from happier days.

Old Simfa sat in the fire light telling the old stories.

"There was a time long ago when the weather was always the same. The days were always the same temperature. The herbs and roots could always be found in the same places. Fruits and nuts grew on the trees already ripe. Animals

walked into the camp to be slain and eaten. Life was so easy that nobody of the Kakass ever really did anything.

It was very boring.

One day the gods met and decided that the Kakass were alive but not really living. Something must be changed.

So the gods made the seasons.

The gods made spring so new growth would make the Kakass glad. From barren emptiness would come living treasures. The grass grew lush in the meadows. Leaves grew to cover bare branches. Birds appeared by magic to fill the silence with music. Where there were ponds the frogs sang. The grazing animals gave birth to their young which jumped and ran and played. The Kakass saw and heard and smelled and were happy.

But spring could not last forever. The frantic growth sapped spring of its strength and spring died.

So the gods made summer to make the Kakass grateful. Fruits and berries and nuts grew to be food which was gathered. In the ponds and streams the fish swam to be caught. The animals grew and became fat and were there to be hunted. The Kakass saw and tasted and ate and were thankful.

But summer could not last forever. The fruits and nuts were all picked leaving the branches bare. The fish swam into the deep waters and could not be reached. The grazing animals gathered in their herds and wandered away. The days and nights grew cold and of a chill summer died.

So the gods made winter to make the Kakass wise. Frost and snow came to make the fire important. The grass did not grow and the trees stayed bare. Ice covered the still waters and the cold made the streams slow to a trickle. Some animals *had left but some stayed and grew thick fur to make warm and comfortable sleeping furs and weatherproof clothing. The Kakass watched and learned how important it was to prepare for times of scarcity.*

But spring came back and heated the days and from a fever winter died.

And so there are three seasons and they follow one another in a circle. And the Kakass are always busy preparing for the next season. They have no time to be bored.

And such is the world and so the Kakass live."

The following day he realized he had not eaten yet. Taking both spears and his digging stick he set out to hunt but his path went first to a lower elevation where he could find moist areas. Here he wandered for a time gathering leafy plants. When he had enough he sought out a comfortable spot and ate a salad.

Salads are delicious but do not have the satisfying solidity of meat. He did have enough to keep him going but it stimulated a deeper appetite. He knew of a mineral lick not far away. That place would be today's destination.

Approaching the spot quietly and from downwind, he soon confirmed that there were no visitors at the lick. This was not a surprise nor was it disheartening. An animal does not need to visit a lick often. Still, most grazers visit the mineral licks from time to time. If you stay silently near the lick sooner or later something will come. It may take several days, but the prey will come.

Predators do not use the mineral licks except as places to hunt. In the past Daganu had wondered why such a difference should exist. On this day he focussed only on the actual hunt.

While he was waiting, Daganu scanned the ground for not only tracks but also for edible plants. He moved very slowly as he collected some. Prey watch for movement above all else. He never forgot that his primary goal was meat. Still, only a fool ignores the food that does not run away. Some of the plants growing around him were known to have fat tubers beneath the ground. They might be a bit bland, but there were ways of dealing with that.

It did not take long to fill his largest pouch with tubers. He filled another with the leafy salad greens. He also picked a spare handful of other herbs, ones that were not precisely nourishing but which did have pleasing flavours.

Then he chose a comfortable place to lay in wait, and prepared to remain until evening. If it was a long wait he could snack on the tubers. They were much better cooked but would satisfy a hungry hunter if eaten raw.

Time passed.

He was considering whether to eat some tubers when he noticed a flicker of movement. A small deer was approaching alone. The situation was ideal. Groups of animals are harder to hunt than solo prey. There are more eyes to watch, more ears to hear and more noses to smell.

The deer came to the mineral lick along a game trail, exactly as Daganu had expected. It approached casually but not carelessly.

Reaching the lick area, it stood for a while, just looking, listening and smelling. When it could not detect any danger it gave its tail a flick and proceeded to lick the soil. Daganu did not know why the soil at this place was food to his prey. In the past he had sampled the soil himself. It tasted like ordinary dirt.

Daganu allowed it time to go about its business. Frequently a deer will make its first spot check for danger soon after it begins to feed.

The deer's head came up, glanced about and went back down.

Daganu was close. He was frequently amazed at how near he could get to his target if only he hid before it arrived, and if he remained motionless until it was occupied in some way. Slowly and silently, he rose. Then he cast his throwing spear.

The deer detected the motion of throwing, but it was too late. The spear struck and entered its rib cage.

Daganu watched the spear bob up and down as the deer ran for the shelter of the forest, but it went down before reaching it.

He waited a little longer before approaching the downed animal. It is best to give a speared animal enough time to finish dying. Sometimes a prey animal will still have enough life within it to rise and run again, or even to fight back. Some overeager hunters collect a series of injuries until they learn this basic lesson. Daganu was not one of those hunters, and in any case the deer never moved again.

As always the young hunter first inspected the killing wound. Some neglect to do this, saying, "The animal's dead. What more do you need?"

But the best hunters never finish learning. It is at these times that you can detect a tendency for your spear to strike a little to the side of your aim point or some other small error. Once detected an error can be addressed and fixed.

The next thing to do was to place some leaves into the mouth of the animal and thank it for the gift of its life. Lack of respect may lead to the spirit of the animals being more reluctant to stand still for the spear when it is cast.

With his hand on the deer's head, Daganu said, "Atta, god of the hunt, thank you for blessing my spear. Please care for the soul of this deer."

At this time it was appropriate to begin the butchering process.

In this case the butchering was very simple. Normally Daganu would take the animal apart and begin the laborious process of transporting every edible part to the Kakass encampment.

But there was no encampment. There were no Kakass.

Daganu shook himself out of immobility. He had a stone knife in a sheath on his belt which he drew.

One of the best large pieces of meat for his purposes is a hind leg. It is easy to remove and easy to carry. It is also the most one hunter can comfortably eat before the meat begins to spoil. A front shoulder is easier to remove but holds less meat.

He left the hide on the leg. It would protect the meat from flies and dirt. He also had another use for it.

Standing after he had finished Daganu looked around. He was not the only predator in these parts. He saw no threats but did see two ravens perched in the nearest tree tops. They were watching him with great interest.

"Hello brother raven," he said. "Here is a feast for you. Please enjoy."

Ravens are a hunter's friend and will follow him. At other times they will alert the hunter to a carcass with their chatter. The easiest of all hunting methods is to scavenge some other predator's kill.

On occasion they will even follow food animals and mark their presence with calls. More than once Daganu had followed raven calls to a bedded animal.

He picked up his throwing spear and cleaned blood off the shaft and point with a handful of grass. If this simple act is not done then the spear will begin to smell bad.

He picked up all of his gear and then swung the leg over a shoulder and made the walk back to his solitary camp.

It was another evening and this led to the building of another fire.

Daganu had removed the hide that had covered the leg and shaped it into a bag which was now suspended above the fire. Such a bag will not burn if it is not allowed to dry out. He had put water into the bag before hanging it just for this purpose. In the water he put pieces of venison and of tuber. Herbal flavourings completed the stew that was soon cooking. A rawhide bag adds its own flavour to anything it might contain; it is an acquired taste, but Daganu had been eating hide bag cooked foods all his life.

The important thing right now is to control the fire. Smaller fires are much easier to control but need careful supervision. This is seldom an issue for a lone hunter. He has fewer distractions than he would find within a group.

Hunters work as a team, each doing his own task; there is less for each individual to do but the talk and bantering within the group can become a distraction, and some things may be forgotten.

Once more memories returned as he watched the flames.

One of the children had been misbehaving rather badly. Simfa sat in her place of honour beside the night fire. As chief she automatically had become the keeper of the lore, in the form of stories. It was her hope that the child would mend his ways if he realized what was at stake, so she began another tale.

"There was a time long ago when the laws of the Kakass had never been spoken. No one thought to speak of rules because every person always did what was right. The young were cared for and the elders were honoured. If the clan was attacked the hunters put themselves between the attackers and the clan even unto death, and they hunted and brought meat to feed all of the clan. The women learned the lore of plants and found food for the clan. They bore the children and raised them and gave guidance to the clan. The children played together and made many friends. They listened to the elders and did not question what they were told.

But it happened that one of the children decided this was too much of a bother. He did what he wanted without considering if it helped the clan. More importantly, he did not consider if it harmed anyone.

Meat was passed around to be shared, when it came to him he took all of the best and walked away to where he could be apart from the rest and keep all of the best for himself.

When it was time to sleep he took the finest of the furs and would not let any other share in its warmth.

If he found any of the clan in his way he shoved them aside and laughed if they fell.

If he became annoyed with anyone, or if he was simply in a bad mood, he struck them until they would bleed.

The elders tried to guide him but he sneered at them and told them that he did as he wished and they could not stop him.

It became so bad that all the elders met and discussed what could be done.

'We cannot live with this,' said one elder.

'He cannot live with us,' said another.

And it happened that he was cast out.

Without the clan you are not fed.

Without the clan you are not sheltered.

Without the clan you are not protected.

Without the clan you are not human.

After that the young children were told the laws of the Kakass because it was clear that not all will behave as they should without this guidance.

That wayward child was driven away because of his very bad conduct. His humanity had been taken from him. He became just another animal. He was never seen again. It may be that he lived a long lonely life. It may be that he died soon after that.

But no one remembers his name."

"And such is the world and so the Kakass live."

A deep chill ran down Daganu's spine.

He had no clan.

He was no longer human.

THREE

The situation he was in just kept getting worse.

Daganu had never minded being by himself. In fact he had always quite enjoyed it. To one who enjoys the solitude of the lone hunter being alone brings with it a feeling of freedom. But he had never been this alone.

The fire was getting too weak. He automatically fed it. What was he to do now? The laws had not addressed this situation. He would need to find an answer by himself. So many parts of him were numb. The biting insects feasted upon his blood. He did not even notice. The way ahead seemed pointless. Was there even a reason to try to stay alive?

His stomach growled.

Well, that was clear enough. Daganu removed the boiling bag from the fire and hung it from a torn spruce root to cool. He took his improvised tripod away from the fire and set it carefully aside. It felt good to be doing something. Keeping busy helped. If you always have something to do then you can deflect the awful emptiness inside.

When the stew had cooled enough Daganu ate. He didn't notice that it tasted good. He was too deep in thought.

So, he wasn't human any more. He was just another animal. He had watched animals all his life. He had studied them. Animals do not lie around feeling morose. They get on with what needs to be done next. He had frequently seen them playing. They had fun.

All right, maybe having fun was too much to ask for.

But there was no need to simply curl up and die. He had been alone on the hunt for many days at a time. Everything he really needed for survival was something he could do. He realized that his philosophy of Just Do It applied to this mess, too. Living as an animal might not be all that bad.

He could always curl up and die later.

He crawled into his shelter and wrapped himself in his furs. He knew he would not be able to sleep with this dilemma spinning inside his mind, but there was nothing else to be done.

But he did sleep. When he woke the sun was shining. He was not going to just stay here. Where should he go? More options than usual were before him because he need not worry about going too far to be able to carry meat back to…

He didn't want to finish that thought.

Hunters like to share their stories. If you pay attention you can learn much from the experience of others. Sometimes it is as if another hunter's stories are your own memories. There was a place three valleys over said to be favoured by the great deer. He had always revelled in the challenge of bringing down a great deer on his own. The task required great skill and total concentration. He could use something that fully occupied his thoughts. Besides, he had never been there.

It was decided. With real purpose, Daganu packed his small amount of gear. He inspected the bindings of the stone points on his spears. He sliced the meat from the hind leg of the deer he had killed the day before and filled his deer hide boiling bag; transforming it into large travel pouch. It could be turned back into a boiling bag later.

Confirming that the fire had safely died the night before, he turned his back to his camp and never thought of it again.

He found a game trail heading vaguely the way he wished to go and followed it. Game trails are paths that have been made by the animals as they travel from one place to another.

The animals are not stupid; they travel the path that is easiest. What a hunter needs to do is remain aware of the direction the trail is heading. Animals do not necessarily wish to go to the same places that hunters do. If a trail deflects too far from the desired direction you should find another that does better and follow it instead. While this method does not always work, on this day it performed admirably. In a surprisingly short time Daganu was climbing into the first mountain pass of this new journey.

As he approached the tree line, he decided to take a break beside a clear trickle of water. He ate his remaining greens and then feasted on slices of raw venison. He drank his fill and then leaned back against a boulder, totally relaxed, to enjoy the view.

There are people who never notice such things. Their heads are too full of their own grubby little concerns, or such was Daganu's opinion. Fortunately, Daganu was not to be numbered among them. The vista before him was magnificent. The mountain slopes on the far side of the valley were mottled with patches of forest and meadow. Various birds soared high overhead or dashed madly from one patch of shrubs to another. A ground squirrel watched him suspiciously.

It was fortunate that he was still capable of enjoying such things.

He reflexively eyed the clouds to determine their direction of travel. A problem became apparent. In the distance was a bank of heavy grey cloud and it was coming straight toward him. He promptly stood up. A mountain pass is not the best place to endure a squall. It could rain, sleet or even snow on him. It was time to continue the trek.

All travellers in that time and place stayed alert to potential dangers, and so it was that Daganu saw the sow bear and her cubs before getting too close. He hoped that she would not notice him.

But there is an old saying among the Kakass; *Wish for food or hunt. Just one of these will starve.* Wishing would not remove danger. Taking appropriate action would. He began to slowly move back the way he had come.

The mother bear saw him. She stood tall on her hind legs for a better view. Her head moved gently back and forth as she tried to catch his scent. Daganu promptly turned sideways and allowed his shoulders to slump. He carefully did not look directly at her. This posture communicates with an animal that you are not a threat and that you are, in fact, submissive. Animals send large amounts of information to one another by use of posture.

The bear remained uncertain. She began to walk slowly toward him.

For his part Daganu walked slowly backward. He took the bag of meat from his shoulder and dropped it on the trail but never stopped backing away.

When she reached that place the mother bear inspected the bag. Discovering it to be food, her interest in Daganu declined. The cubs, which had followed their mother closely, fell upon the bag and tried to wrest it from their mother's possession. Mother bear's interest in Daganu disappeared almost entirely.

Daganu continued to retreat until he judged that he was safely distant. He walked well off to the side – the downwind side – and resumed his journey. He had essentially paid the bear a toll to let him pass.

When he crossed a trickle of water, too small to be called a stream, he paused and filled his water bladder. It filled slowly, but he was not familiar with the land ahead, and he did not know how frequent streams would be. Water was heavy, but thirst was a greater concern.

The cloud bank he had seen continued to drift nearer, but Daganu managed to enter the forest well ahead of it. Moving downslope he found a large spruce tree with thick branches. This tree would not shed all the rain, but it would be enough to make a major difference.

Since he had time before the rain began Daganu collected low hanging branches from nearby trees. These he placed among the lower branches of his chosen shelter tree thereby improving its ability to shed water, and the tree became an umbrella.

When the rain started Daganu was comfortably seated with his back to the trunk of his tree. He was confident that he would remain dry, if not fully shielded from wind. He settled himself and adjusted his day furs to be as snug as possible. So long as he remained still the furs would keep him warm against the humid chill of the night. No hunter carried night furs while on the hunt except in winter. They were too heavy.

It rained fitfully for the rest of the daylight and into the dark. Then it settled down to a steady, drumming soaker. Daganu slept.

Morning light found the rain still falling steadily. There is not much that you can do to change the weather. Some of the clan had tried to influence the gods into doing precisely that. The gods took their offerings, but did nothing. Daganu did not bother trying. Even if he had wanted to, the bear had eaten all of his remaining food. He was left with nothing to offer. So he sat under the tree and watched the rain. The Kakass occasionally missed meals or went unfed for a day or more. This was inconvenient, but it was not a big deal.

What did bother him was when he felt the need to defecate. People of the Kakass urinated casually wherever they happened to be; within reason, of course. Bowel movements were not permitted within the grounds of an encampment. Daganu spent some time selecting a lavatory tree. It needed to be nearby and also to shed most of the rain. Being downwind would be a bonus. As it turned out there was a suitable tree close by, and he was soon comfortable again.

It rained all day.

It rained the next day too.

Daganu really wished the bear had not taken his food. Water was not an issue. He drank whenever he felt like it, and so his water bladder would not become drained he refilled it frequently from the trickle that was being shed by his shelter tree. It was very slow, but he had nothing else to do.

There were no food plants that Daganu could recognize near the tree shelter. He wasn't hungry enough to wander off into the rain to look for food that might not be there. The risk of getting a deep chill outweighed any likely benefit.

Tomorrow he might change his mind, but the next day the sky was clear.

With nothing to hold him back Daganu started out as soon as the visibility improved to the point where there was no risk of stumbling over unseen hazards. The first part of the journey was all downhill. By midday he had reached the river on the valley floor. There was always a river on the valley floor, or at least that was Daganu's experience.

His experienced eye noticed a side channel that was quite shallow at both ends with a slightly deeper middle section. He went to the upstream end and placed a barrier of rocks across it. The water still flowed through but a fish would have great difficulty passing it.

He then went downstream, detouring far enough away from the deeper water to be sure that he would not spook any fish, and did the same thing there.

Walking carefully beside the isolated deeper section he then looked for fish. There was no guarantee that any fish were held within it. If not, all his work would have been wasted, but he was lucky. He spied several shadows moving within the water. Most of the time a shadow is all you can see of a fish underwater.

Fish are difficult to catch by hand, even when trapped, so Daganu intended to use a spear. He would not, however, use either of his hunting spears. Their stone points were far too valuable to risk breaking them against rocks.

There was a stand of young willows not far from the river. There are many kinds of willows. Some are twisted and gnarled while others grow straight. He could see from a distance that these willows were of a suitably straight variety.

It did not take long to find a willow of an acceptable girth which grew up to a narrow fork. His hand axe cut the willow easily. Using his axe he sharpened both tips of the fork. The idea was that he would stab at the fish. One or the other of the two forks would puncture fish. It couldn't hold the fish reliably by itself but should be able to pin it against the bottom long enough for Daganu's hand to grip it. At least that was the plan.

And to his satisfaction, that is what did happen. Daganu came away from the river with three fish. Fish are easy to cook. They can also be eaten raw. Daganu was hungry. He ate the first fish raw.

That evening, not far from the next pass, he cooked the other two, and he remembered to make a proper offering to the gods. For some of his earlier meals he had forgotten to give the gods their due. He consoled himself by thinking that animals probably did not need to make offerings. It was the first time that he had actually found that being an animal could be an advantage.

He was through the second pass well before midday. The travelling was easier here than in the other places he had been. The slope leading down from the pass was gentler and the forest was not as dense. He could see farther here. He could see something interesting some distance away to his right. What looked like a gap in the land itself snaked its way down the mountain slope to the valley bottom. He wondered what it could be.

He stood still for a time pondering this mystery. Then he shook his head. Why not go and see? He didn't have much else but he did have time and freedom. He changed his destination.

As he neared the gash he saw that it was a narrow, steep sided canyon. This presented intriguing possibilities; he had found good things in canyons before. He regarded them as places of good magic. It seemed that anything could happen at the bottom of a canyon.

He made his way to the edge so he could see that bottom. He expected to see a river or a stream. He did not.

It did look like there had once been a river flowing there, but no water remained. He did not know that rivers sometimes shift their flows. Had he considered it he would have realized that the river below the last camp of the Kakass was now dammed so that it would need to find a different route; but he avoided thinking about that camp and that slide. It was hurt too much. It would be a very long time before he could think about it without feeling great pain.

In the meantime, he considered the sight before him. Something more was different with the bottom. Dry river beds were not uncommon in some places. They flowed in the spring only. For the rest of the year they were trails of smoothed rocks. This one had some rocks showing, but not many. It was more sand than rock and it was unusually flat. Why?

He walked the edge of the canyon moving downhill. He looked into it at intervals; and then he smelled a familiar heavy aroma. Nothing else smelled like that. There were mammoths in the canyon!

Cautiously he approached the edge. Slowly he peered down. He could see them. From where he was laying he saw eight of the huge shaggy animals. No, there were nine! From beneath one of the mammoths came a baby. It was clearly in high spirits. Mammoths don't actually run, but this calf was doing its best to try. With its trunk held high it scampered, as much as a mammoth can scamper, up the canyon floor and back. From time to time it stopped and looked back at its mother as if to make sure she was watching. It…

A flicker of movement disrupted Daganu's train of thought. There was something else in the canyon. What was it? It moved again and suddenly Daganu could clearly see the source.

Longtooth! It was a huge cat, mottled brown, with enormous canine teeth that dropped well below the great cat's lower jaw. Its camouflage was so good that even from his high vantage point Daganu had been unaware of it until it moved. His attention had been focussed on the mammoth calf - as was the longtooth's.

Daganu nearly shrugged his shoulders. This would have communicated to any human hunter with him, no! Do not! Mammoths were not safe prey even for the master of all predators. He studied it to understand why it would take such a risk.

The cat was very thin. Daganu could see its ribs clearly beneath its hide. And he saw why it was in such poor condition. Its left hind leg was badly injured, perhaps even broken. It was in a desperate dilemma.

He saw the great cat's muscles tense as the mammoth calf came near, and then relax as the calf went back to its mother. Mother and child touched each other with their trunks. Then the calf moved away from safety, closer and closer to the sudden death hiding behind a large rock. It approached too closely. The cat pounced and with one quick motion bit deeply into the mammoth calf's throat. The calf squealed in pain and terror as the mighty teeth penetrated flesh and severed the carotid arteries.

The entire herd of mammoths thundered to the rescue, enraged that some predator dared to attack one of their own. The sabretooth snarled and held his ground. It needed this meal so badly, it did not turn to run until the very last moment.

It had forgotten to make allowance for the injury to its hind leg. Rather than make the powerful leap the cat had intended the damaged leg collapsed. It scrambled back to its feet but the brief delay allowed the mammoths to reach it. Screaming their fury they trampled and smashed the feline body. It probably was dead within seconds but merely killing it was not enough. The herd wanted to reduce the cat to a soggy mess.

Then it was over.

The mammoths, led by the mother, went back to the dead calf. When they were gathered around it they caressed it with their trunks. Mammoths are intelligent enough to understand what death is. In their own way they mourned the loss of a precious infant.

After much time had passed, the herd moved away up the canyon - all except for the mother. She remained by her baby a while longer. Then she raged back to the fallen cat and trampled it some more.

In time, even she walked away.

When he was quite sure the mammoths were not returning Daganu carefully climbed down to the canyon floor. He remained on high alert in case they did return. He went first to the body of the calf. He quickly sliced through the hide and removed as much of the meat as he thought he could carry. Then he moved over to what was left of the cat.

Few bones were unbroken. The skull was shattered. To his surprise the giant canines remained intact. He removed them and tucked them into a belt pouch. This was much easier than he had expected. The skull was so badly broken that the tooth sockets no longer anchored the teeth solidly.

Lifting the meat he proceeded to carefully carry it to the top of the canyon wall. It took several trips. He was relieved when he reached the top for the last time. Only now did he feel safe from the mammoth herd.

The ravens were gathering, and several circled Daganu. "Down there," he told them with a gesture.

They flew down as if following his instructions. There was plenty to share but ravens are not the highest ranking scavengers. They intended to fill their bellies before the eagles and other, larger predators arrived.

Daganu carried his mammoth meat to a suitable stand of trees. There he built a shelter. There he would stay until he had smoked and dried all of meat.

That night he sat by the fire with his belly as full as he could ever remember. He stared into the flames and pondered what he had seen. Mammoths cared greatly for their children. Not only the mother cared, but the entire herd cared. If one member of the herd should be attacked and killed, the entire herd thirsted for revenge. When a member of the herd died each surviving member of the herd mourned. The mammoth herd was as much a clan as the Kakass had been.

As he sat in the dark forest watching the flames of his fire Daganu reached a decision: he would not live the rest of his life as a wild thing alone in the world. He would find some way to join a clan and thus return a deeper meaning to his existence.

Daganu would become human again.

FOUR

In the morning Daganu began the enormous task of preserving the meat. Mammoth meat was a delicacy and he intended to dine on it as long as he could. He found three small trees of the correct size and cut them down. He stripped them of their branches and arranged them in a triangle. Using some of the grass cord that he had braided earlier that year he lashed poles to the trees at roughly waist height. On this base he lashed slender shafts across the frame and parallel to one another. The shafts were one fist width apart. From a distance it looked like a platform he could stand upon. It was nowhere near strong enough to be used in that way, but that did not matter. That was only what it looked like from a distance, not what it was intended to be. This was a drying and smoking rack. He added two more levels of drying racks built in the same way as the first.

The ground beneath the rack was covered by dry, leafy material. This needed to be scraped away until the soil beneath it was bare. Daganu would later make a smoky fire here and precautions must be taken to contain that fire. If it escaped it would travel far and consume a great deal of wood both dead and living; that would be undesired to say the least.

Now Daganu sliced the meat into strips as thin as he could manage which he draped across the slender shafts, taking care to maintain a space between them. He also tried to remove all of the fat. Left on, the fat can go rancid. He ran out of room on the rack long before he ran out of meat. He would need to repeat the process several times.

You cannot use just any kind of wood for a smoking fire. Trees with narrow needle-like leaves are not suitable for this task because within the smoke of these trees is a tar that forms a deposit on every surface that is bathed in its smoke. Meat smoked in this way develops a flavour that is very unpleasant. You must instead take only wood from trees with wide, flat leaves. These are the trees whose leaves change colour and fall from the trees before each winter.

Daganu wondered why the gods made them that way. He supposed it marked them so the Kakass could identify which woods to use for smoking and which woods were good only for building and fires. There are many kinds of wood to be found in a forest and each imparts a different flavour to meat or fish preserved by its smoke. Choosing wood for taste and balancing time of smoking for depth of flavour is complicated. Daganu could preserve meat but had little control over the finer points. The real artists of the smoker were the women.

The fire should be mostly coals to smoke the meat well. Some heat should reach the meat but not enough to actually cook it, only dry it. Using green wood will increase the amount of smoke produced. Dry wood gets a better result, at least in the opinions of the Kakass, but Daganu was more interested in saving time.

Once he had his smoking fire burning, being careful not to allow much in the way of flame, Daganu stepped back and studied the results judiciously. They were satisfactory.

He then went into the deep forest.

There are patterns to be found everywhere in nature. For example, some broad leaved trees have leaves and twigs that spring from the branches in a spiral. If you stack such branches, then the pile you make will be light and airy. This was an excellent technique if you were making a bed, but did not contain smoke very well. Others have leaves that only grow out from the sides of the twigs. These tend to be shrubs growing beneath a canopy of trees.

Daganu collected a large amount of leafy branches from the appropriate plants. Bringing them back to the smoking rack he laid them one at a time to form a wall around the outside of the tripod. The leaves that lay flat upon each other formed a barrier holding the smoke in. This would speed up the smoking process. The same twigs and branches made a screen to protect the fire and smoke from wind gusts.

Now Daganu settled in for a long wait.

He must maintain a watch over the fire, keeping it burning but not too hot, while watching the smoke to see that it swirls among the meat strips and is not blown away by a changing wind.

But mostly you wait.

While he waited for the meat to smoke, he gathered materials and made a sturdy basket. Most hunters learned basket weaving. Big pieces of meat can be easily carried, but smaller pieces cannot. You either abandoned all the small pieces or make a container, and making a basket did not take long.

He still felt the need to do something. Several days and just sitting under a tree had not been fun. He opened the pouch containing the two enormous killing teeth of the dead cat and looked at them.

He held them in his hand and looked at them.

He laid them on the ground and looked at them.

He walked circles around them and looked at them.

He remembered noticing certain stones on his path down the canyon side to where the mammoth calf had lain. All Kakass children were trained to observe their surroundings as they moved through the world. Daganu had recognized the stones as tool mother stones, these stones which could be carefully shaped into axes, knives, and similar tools. They were not of the best quality – flint was supreme – but there was no flint to be found in Kakass territory. All the flint used by his clan was carried in from far away by traders. The Kakass did not even know what direction the flint came from.

Hunters are trained in the arts of tool- making but none are allowed to make anything from flint until they have sufficient mastery for shaping mother stone. Mother stones could be found in pockets throughout Kakass territory; flint was sourced only from traders, came from far away and was precious. One learned on less valuable materials.

He checked the fire, made a few minor adjustments, and walked back to the canyon. He peered over the edge. Ravens and other scavengers squabbled over the mammoth calf remains. Several looked up at him, but he wasn't nearly as interesting as food. They rejoined the argument.

Daganu did not need to climb far down the canyon wall to find some mother stones that were the size he had wanted. He cracked them against each other to see if they would break. The first few did not, but it was not long until he had a handful of fragments of a size that pleased him. He filled one of his belt pouches with them. He took them back to the smoking fire.

He took off his day furs, laid them bare side up on the ground and placed upon it the newly gathered stone fragments and the teeth. He carefully inspected the stones and made a selection. He lifted one of the giant teeth and he poked at it with a finger. This action didn't do anything to the tooth but it helped him select a spot to begin drilling a hole.

He picked a stone with a good, sharp point, and held the point against the point against the spot he had selected. It was near base of the tooth. He began scratching. For a while it seemed that nothing was happening, but eventually he thought he could feel a depression forming.

Occasionally he felt the need to get up, stretch and walk around. At these times he checked the fire and the meat. If either the fire or the meat was not behaving as he wished he made any necessary alterations before returning to his other project.

By the time he had made a clearly visible saucer shape on the tooth he had worn out several of the stones. He might need to make a trip back to his stone mine in the canyon to gather more. But that time had not yet come.

He made another inspection of the smoking fire. This time he spent a little more time inspecting everything as it might be longer than usual before he came back. He did not go back to his work station but headed into the forest. He was looking for some fire drill sticks, extra thin and extra hard if he could get them. He wanted to drill a small hole completely through the tooth and he had no intention of wearing out the drill he used to make his fires.

The search took a long time but he did manage to find some thin and dry sticks made from very hard wood.

That was all he could manage to get done on the first day. While he had to stay awake to tend the fire and the meat, it became too dark to continue with his other project.

He had to remind himself that the important thing was the meat even though preparing the teeth was much more interesting.

Morning came once more. Daganu decided that the first batch of meat was both sufficiently smoked and dried. He removed it from the drying racks and replaced it with fresh strips.

As the second batch proceeded to smoke, he began the second stage of work on the tooth. He took one of the new fire drill sticks, dipped the tip into some sandy soil, and set the point into the depression that he had made. He began to spin it as if he was trying to start a fire using the tooth in place of the fireboard. The depression was deep enough that he could keep the drill tip inside it. The sand provided grit which helped the drill grind a hole into the tooth.

As he spun the fire drill the tooth did not catch fire, but the part directly under the drill point became very hot. The heat caused the spot under the drill point to become brittle. As time passed the sand wore through and eventually Daganu had cut a hole all the way through the tooth.

He leaned back and allowed himself a well-earned rest. Then he began the whole process once more using the other tooth.

By the time the last of the meat was safely processed Daganu was wearing both teeth around his neck suspended by a length of braided grass cord.

He was so glad to be done. He was tired of being enslaved to tending the fire. He didn't know how Bathen did it - spending all of his nights keeping the fire healthy. Actually, he mused, that task was totally different. Bathen was working for the good of the entire clan. Daganu was merely working.

He didn't want to be an animal. He must regain what he had lost.

Was that even possible? Those people of the clan that the mountain had eaten would never be coming back. They could not be regained. Could he start a new clan? Such a thing was known to happen. Sometimes a clan grew too numerous for their territory to support them. At such times part of the clan could go a different direction from the main group. If they could find a territory that would support them; then they could begin building a clan of their own.

No, that was looking down the wrong marmot hole. The problem now was not having too many in the clan. There was no one at all.

He sat by the ash of the dead fire and brooded, and a random thought floated by; here were other clans.

Normally when clans met they kept their distance and shouted insults while brandishing weapons. If one clan was well inside the other's territory its nerve would break and then the offender would flee.

Alternatively, there were times when the meeting happened on turf not strongly claimed by either group. These were the times when the shouting would fade away and instead they would regard each other with suspicion which could potentially lead to curiosity. Sometimes curiosity reached the point where individuals would try to communicate. This connection could lead to those same individuals inspecting each other's weapons. If that happened then trade began.

On those happy occasions the animosity died and friendships formed. Subsequent meetings were likely to be peaceful, and, if they were allowed to develop, there would be limited exchanges of members. In later times this became known as intermarriage.

However, that didn't really apply to Daganu's dilemma.

He retired to the simple camp he had been using though the mammoth smoking period. He had a raging tension headache, and he realized that he would be no travelling today.

Daganu had been able to sleep. He woke feeling much better: physically better, at any rate.

He began to wonder if clans ever adopted wanderers. He didn't know. He couldn't remember it happening.

If only old Simfa was here to ask! Well, if you cannot ask an elder, then find out for yourself.

He knew of several different clans, so he had to choose from among them. The most important consideration must be how likely they were to allow him to join them.

Closest to the Kakass would be the Kakass Vag. Kakass meant "people," and vag meant "nearly." Combined into "Kakass Vag" the meaning became "almost people," or "those most like us." One of Daganu's friends had once told him that the Kakass Vag had split from the Kakass a long time ago. He had no idea how his friend had learned that. It could not be from his own experience because his friend was the same age as Daganu. If the only information you have is not reliable it is still, however, your only information. Daganu would try to find the Kakass Vag.

At least they would not try to kill him on first sight - no one did that. A lone traveller was not much of a threat. More importantly, a lone traveller might be a trader. Traders were valuable people. No place was ever the source of everything you wanted. In the case of the Kakass, traders were the only source of top quality tool stone. Local stone could be worked in tools and spear points but those tools did not last very long, and those spear points were never as sharp as those made with the stone the traders carried.

Daganu had wondered many times just where that stone came from. Every time he had raised the subject in conversation the response had always been the same. *Who cares? They come from the traders.*

Were traders human? That was an interesting thought. If they were, perhaps the easiest way to regain his humanity would be to become a trader. Two problems, however, occurred to him. First, he had nothing to trade. As problems go, that was a big one. He could imagine carrying flint to the clans in this area, but he had nothing to exchange in order to get the flint to carry. Second, he had no idea where the flint might be found or even where the traders came from. These were serious flaws in any plan to become a trader.

He was beginning to feel dizzy.

It was time to focus on one thing only. He would try to find the Kakass Vag. They were said to normally be to the sunward of where the Kakass had roamed. He must go sunward.

Daganu considered his location: he was at the crest of a pass. Both of the valleys connected by the pass showed exits to the sunward. If he went sunward up the valley he was currently in, would that take him to Kakass Vag territory? Or would it take him further away? Would he need to walk all the way back to where he was now? If only he actually knew something!

Old Simfa was bathed in the golden glow of the fire.

"There was a time long ago, not in this valley, when the world was new, that the Kakass were still learning about the world. They had learned how to hunt and had learned how

to gather. They had learned how to survive each season in turn. They had learned how to make fire and had learned how to cook and how to smoke meat. They had learned much.

A young hunter was bragging, as young men sometimes do. 'We have learned so much that we already know everything!' The gods sometimes listened to the Kakass speak around the fire in those days. They were listening then. They were not pleased. Through the flames they spoke to the young hunter. 'You do not know everything. Your boasting offends. We shall give you a task. Find a cave and learn what it is for.' The young hunter felt the rebuke. 'I am ashamed,' he said. 'I will do as you command. But please tell me this one thing; what is a cave?' But the gods had gone.

The young hunter turned to the chief. 'I do not know what a cave is,' he said. 'Can you tell me?'

'I cannot,' she replied. 'It is something we have yet to learn.'

The young hunter turned to the keeper of the night fire. 'I do not know what a cave is,' he said. 'Can you help me?'

'I cannot,' he replied. 'That is your task.'

The young hunter lowered his head. 'I will do the best that I can,' he said, 'though I do not know how to begin.'

In the morning he left the camp to find out what a cave was and what it was for.

He walked a long time. He asked every animal he met, 'Do you know what a cave is?'

Every animal he met said, 'No.'

And it happened that as he was walking near a place where the hillside was steep, and he saw a hole in the slope.

He looked into the hole. It went into the hillside farther than he could see, so he went into it. As he moved further in, away from the entrance, the light became dimmer and dimmer.

Our sight was better in those days. The young hunter could see in the darkness. He saw a bear pressing its paw against the wall. When its paw came away it had made a track that remained.

'Oh, bear,' said the young hunter, 'what is this thing you do?'

'Oh, hunter,' said the bear, 'you and I now stand inside the very flesh of the Earth Mother. I leave my mark on the wall of this cave so that the Earth Mother will know who I am and will remember my people.'

'Is this a cave?' the young hunter asked.

'It is,' the bear replied.

'And should I leave my mark on the wall as you do?'

'If you want the Earth Mother to remember your people and care for them, you should.'

And the young hunter pressed his hand to the wall and when his hand came away a hand print remained. We can no longer do this. We have to use paint.

The young hunter returned to the clan. That night by the fire he told the people what he had learned. 'A cave is an entrance into the very flesh of the Earth Mother,' he said, 'and it is a holy place. If you leave your marks on the wall the Earth Mother will know you and will remember you and your people.

'And I learned one more thing. If you must begin something and you know nothing about it, just begin.'

And such is the way of the world and so the Kakass live."

Daganu turned to the direction of the newly risen sun. The Kakass Vag lived to the sunward. He did not know anything more. If you must begin something and you know nothing about it, just begin. He began to walk across the pass.

FIVE

A s he walked, Daganu constantly scanned the surrounding area for edible or useful plants; he also watched the ground for tracks. This continual observation is a reflex action that all Kakass do. He came to a sudden stop when he recognized a plant he knew as washing weed. In the parlance of the Kakass the word "weed" denoted any plant that is both not a tree and one you did not want to eat.

If you picked washing weed and crushed the plant in water, then the plant would produce slippery foam that helped remove dirt and grime.

Daganu, after days of working amid smoke and ash, was sticky with dried sweat and crusted with spruce needles, and reeked of smoke. He really wanted a bath, and so he collected a suitable supply of washing weed and changed his direction toward the river flowing through the valley bottom.

He did not want to bathe in the river itself, the water in a mountain river is always cold. However, there frequently are small isolated ponds near a river. A small, shallow pond can warm up to a truly pleasant degree.

After a search he found such a pond. It even had a sandy bottom - it was perfect.

Daganu dropped all of his gear near the pond's edge and waded in. After reaching approximately the depth of his knees the water seemed to be at its deepest point. He sat down and blissfully lay onto his back. Here he simply relaxed.

It felt so good.

He soaked in the sunlight until he forgot about his washing weed and allowed his hand to open. Realizing that he had released the weed, he sat up and retrieved it before it could drift too far away or disperse.

He rubbed the weed against itself in the water until he had thin suds which he worked into his hair. When he judged that he had done enough scrubbing he took the weed and rubbed it directly onto his body. He was thorough. He made certain that he had not missed any spots before rinsing himself. The grimy sweat had been truly uncomfortable but now it was gone. Daganu felt so much better, refreshed and reenergized.

He arranged his hair the best he could, but he did not do this often. There had always been young women who seemed eager to do it for him and they did a far better job than he could. After finishing with him the young women would gather together to whisper and giggle. He had decided that it was best if he did not know what they said.

He missed that. There was so much that he missed.

It was time to move on.

He walked the game trails heading vaguely sunward. As ever he scanned the trail for sign.

He saw a mound on the trail ahead. His ears perked up. Well, figuratively. They would have perked for real if he had been a wolf. Of course, if he was a wolf he wouldn't even be on this trail. He…

He shrugged his shoulders. Enough! Just take a look at the pile of animal poop.

He felt a familiar excitement build as he realized it was the scat of a great deer and that the tracks suggested it was a bull. By the feel of the scat it was really fresh and was still warm.

He stood still and scanned what he could see of the area, trying to see it from the point of view of the animal. If I was this animal, where might I be going?

Then he felt himself slowly deflate. He was already carrying as much meat as he wished to be burdened with. He considered his options. The Kakass Vag were not waiting for him. They didn't even know he existed. He could hunt this animal, and if he killed it he could camp beside it until he had eaten so much that his load of meat would be equal to what he already had.

That made no sense at all.

Well, then.

He didn't phrase his decision with actual words. He didn't want to.

He continued to walk the trail.

Moving on did not mean he no longer watched the trail exactly as before. There were many reasons to watch for sign. Some smaller animals would be welcome to eat fresh, not dried and smoked. Fresh meat would also extend the time his preserved rations would last. One of the lessons learned by all the clans was that times of famine *did* happen. Never reject fresh food if it is available.

Of more importance was the possibility the trail had been used by bears, great cats, wolves and the like. Bears and cats he had already met on this trip, but to think there would be no more predators nearby because he had already encountered them all was a fool's wishful thinking. Of paramount importance was the chance that he would find human tracks. He wanted to be the first to discover any such tracks so if there was a meeting it was of his choosing.

Off to the side he heard the croak of a raven and he made a note of where it came from. One call meant nothing, but sometimes when the raven called again and again it was telling the world about meat. The meat might be another predator's kill or it might be an animal still alive and healthy, an animal that the raven wished some predator would come and kill for the bird. Ravens had in the past led Daganu to a good hunting opportunity more than once. Of course the meat might also be the last few shreds remaining on a ribcage.

The raven called again - twice.

Daganu stopped. He looked in the direction of the raven calls.

He looked down the trail.

He looked toward the raven.

He sighed. He had to know.

If raven called because there was an animal that it wanted dead, it was best that you try to please that raven.

It might later speak to you again at a time when you were as hungry as it was.

Daganu did not rush. The walking was not silent today, but there are ways to deal with that. There are methods of walking that sound like other animals, and these do not cause concern. Some of his favourite memories were of sneaking up to a bedded animal and casting his spear into it before it knew he was there. That was a technique which was not for beginners.

The raven called often enough and Daganu was able to follow the sound easily. He did not sneak up on any animal but neither did he hear one run away.

At last he found the raven. It cocked its head and studied Daganu.

It said "Prrrruk!" and flew away.

Daganu shook his head gently, smiled and gestured appreciation for raven's joke. If you don't think ravens have a sense of humour, you haven't met very many ravens.

It was getting late, but Daganu saw a good place to rest. He thought the raven may have selected it for him. Whether or not the bird had meant this was not to be known, but it felt good to feel a part of the great swirl of life around him.

Besides, as was mentioned earlier, Daganu really liked birds.

He had not been inflicted with nightmares, which was a good thing, but he had been having trouble sleeping. He would wake up in the middle of the night and lie very still, waiting for something to happen. In ordinary circumstances he would have arisen and tended the fire, but because he was far outside his known territory he was reluctant to show a light in the darkness.

Most nights when he had been on a normal hunting expedition he would have lit a fire to cook whatever he had killed. These days he would eat salad greens while he walked and in the evenings he ate cold smoked mammoth. It was good, but because he did not need to cook he had no need of a fire. Therefore, he would lie silently and listen to night noises. If he was fortunate he would hear the howling of wolves in the distance.

If he was unfortunate, then he would spend his time listening to the high pitched drone of mosquitos.

If rain came pattering through the trees, then he would stay put in his wrapped snugly in his day furs. His shelters did not always protect him well and on those nights, and some of the days, he was wet and miserable. When he was damp and chilled he would stop where he was and make a fire. Fires can be made in wet conditions; it just takes preparation and a little more skill.

Kakass hunters are trained to notice materials that are good for fire making. As they walk, they see things that would be useful as tinder or as the early fire feeding food. If you can gather the materials while they are dry, and keep them in a waterproof container of some sort, then creating the first small flame is doable. Building the fire up from that point is normally not a problem. Daganu had reflexively collected a good supply of tinders and enough small fire fodder to begin a blaze. There were not many times when his fire making failed.

He was not sure how long he had been scouting for the Kakass Vag. It seemed to have been much more than a moon, but he knew that was not the case.

The forest was large and stretched on forever. He was most likely to find tracks in the wet soils near the river, but he climbed up to the mountain meadows some days to enjoy the views and escape the mosquitoes.

He was up the mountain one day when he saw a wisp of smoke. It was on the other side of the valley - a little distance up the mountainside. He watched it carefully, looking for indications of what, exactly, it was. It did not spread and the trees around it were lushly green. Not a wildfire. It did not change in volume. It was a campfire.

Quite suddenly his whole daily routine was disrupted. His focus had been on looking for any signs of another clan. He was a hunter. He could do that. He had done that, and now his hunt for other people seemed to be over.

He sat quite abruptly on the grass. A sudden thought had stunned him. In all the days of hunting he had never considered *how* he was going to make contact; this was not a minor oversight. Just striding into their camp as if he already belonged there was unthinkable. If anything would alienate him from the people he had found, that would be it. Under no circumstances should he enter the camp during the night. The only beings who would do such a thing were demons or enemy clansmen. A night contact would prove him to be hostile.

Should he build his own fire and allow them to find him? Perhaps so. Of course that would cast doubt over his desire to join their clan. It would be better to be the one taking the initiative.

He decided the best way would be to wait until a hunting party was returning. He still had half a basket of smoked mammoth. He would trail behind them close enough that he appeared to be a straggler from their group, and as he neared the camp he would swing the basket down from its place on his back and set it in front of him. If he then took two steps back and waited he would appear to be no threat and it would be obvious that he was offering the meat as a gift. To offer mammoth meat should set a friendly tone to the meeting. They should at least try to establish communication before trying to kill him.

Very well, that was the plan.

Certainly he should not make the attempt today. He was again in great need of a bath. His plan also depended on following a returning hunting party. He must wait for such a party to leave the camp. By following them at a great distance he would know when they were returning and whether they had been successful. His best chance lay in arriving at the camp with meat after an unsuccessful hunting party returned.

Trailing a party of hunters was risky. They would be on alert for any movement and being discovered would be disastrous. But he was the hunter who could sneak up on a deer in its bed. He could do this.

There was so much to do, and one of his tasks must be to find a good growth of washing weed. He must stay clean in preparation for an attempt to impress the clan. He hoped they were the Kakass Vag. Perhaps he would find out while watching them.

He had no experience with this sort of thing, and, for the first time he became nervous.

Two days passed and no party left. But a party did return. From his point of surveillance Daganu did not see them until they entered the clearing in which the clan camped. By then it was far too late to implement his plan. Those who returned were carrying something but Daganu was too far away to see what it was. It did not seem to be very much.

Any meat seemed to be cause for excitement. That night's fire was larger than usual. There was drumming, singing and dancing. Daganu did not recognize any of the songs, but such a reaction to what appeared to a small amount of meat suggested one of two things.

Perhaps the people had been having difficulty finding enough food to prevent hunger. That threw their skill level into question. If they were having problems just getting enough to eat in a season of plenty they might not be a group he wished to join. On the other hand such a group would view his level of skill as highly valuable. This would make them more likely to welcome him. The other possibility was that this group of people were simply full of the joy of living. That would make them more attractive to him. But which was it?

Daganu sat in his fireless camp and brooded. His plan seemed insufficient. He needed to decide whether to give it a try or whether he should do something different.

When sunrise came, he had already left his cold and uninviting camp. He was at the small pond which he used for his bathing. The water was cold. Nevertheless he washed thoroughly, both hair and body. When he emerged, he was shivering.

The Kakass women used to braid their own hair if the other women were busy. Daganu tried, but his arms did not reach behind his head so well as a woman's. After several tries, he surrendered and settled for having it all hang down his back. He brushed all the grass off his day furs. He made certain the long teeth were hanging properly from a new and unfrayed grass cord. He was as ready as he was going to get.

He felt like he was going to throw up.

Calling all his courage to support him, Daganu walked down the trail. He was the hunter who could walk up to a deer when it was sleeping and not wake it. He was the hunter who single handed hunted the great deer. He was the hunter who had negotiated his passage past a she bear with cubs. He was the hunter who had climbed down a cliff to collect meat from a mammoth calf knowing full well that if the cow mammoth returned, he would have no chance of escape. He could do this.

It wasn't working.

He could now see though the trees to the meadow in which the camp that represented all his hope waited.

He stopped.

He closed his eyes.

He murmured a brief prayer to Atta, god of the hunt.

He began to walk again.

When he first stepped into the clearing no one noticed.

He was close to halfway when someone shouted. Now everybody was looking.

He swung the basket down from his shoulders and held it in front of himself. He had shifted his spears into one hand and with that hand he also grasped the basket. That hand was very full.

It was awkward. He hoped he wouldn't drop anything.

He walked into the camp.

SIX

As he neared the cluster of people nearest the fire he scanned the group. Three elderly women stood near the fire. He approached the one closest to him. He placed the basket of mammoth meat in front of her. He laid his spears beside the basket and took two careful steps backward.

He waited.

The woman studied him briefly. She looked at the basket and then back at his face.

She shrugged 'no' and looked pointedly at another of the old women.

Daganu took two steps forward and lifted the basket again. He left the spears where they were laying. Taking basket to the woman indicated he set it before her. He took two steps back. She studied his face for a time, then stooped and picked up a piece of the cured meat. She regarded it and smelled it. Her eyes widened. "**This is mammoth!**" she exclaimed.

A murmur spread through the crowd.

The chief, for she was such, quickly regained her composure, annoyed with herself that ever she lost it. She now skewered him with her look.

"**Who are you?**" she demanded.

"I am Daganu of the Kakass," Daganu replied. The chief pronounced her words strangely, but he had no difficulty understanding her. This area was only thinly inhabited, and he had never before encountered an accent.

"**Why are you here?**" the chief asked.

"I seek a new place to live."

"**You do not live with your clan?**"

"I cannot."

"**Why? Were you cast out?**"

"I was not cast out. My people are dead."

A louder murmur spread through the crowd.

The chief drew herself more erect. "**Explain this. What clan would do this thing? It is a great evil.**"

Daganu's eyes closed in pain. He rocked lightly on the balls of his feet.

"It was no clan. Do you recall the night the ground shook?"

The people muttered agreement. The chief shook her head. "**I do,**" she said.

"I am a lone hunter. That night I was away from the camp. The ground shook and frightened me. Then there came a great roar of some mighty beast. That was worse."

The chief's eyes narrowed. "**The ground shook. We heard no roaring.**"

"You were fortunate. It turned my belly into water." Daganu visibly struggled to continue. "As soon as there was enough light to see safely, I went back to the camp.

When I got there…" Daganu's breathing was in small, quick breaths, as if he was holding some object of great weight.

"When I got there…I saw…the mountain had eaten my people."

As he stood still in obvious pain, the chief searched for the right words.

"I…your words have little meaning. Did they fall into a cave?"

Daganu shook his head. "The side of the mountain was gone. In its place were only huge rocks, piled high from halfway up the slope where the camp had been, across the valley and to the bottom of the slope on the other side. I spent a day looking for my people." He hung his head. "But I found no sign."

Just like the Kakass, the Kakass Vag were trained from an early age to allow any speaker the time to have their say. This situation, however, was too much. The polite murmuring burst into a cacophonic jumble of urgent questions. All who were speaking demanded their own question should be answered first.

It was a measure of the chief's own discomfiture that at first, she did nothing to regain order. If Daganu was aware of this he did not show it, lost as he was in his own living nightmare. His eyes were closed, and he gently rocked back and forth on his feet.

The hubbub finally began to lose momentum.

"Keeper of the day fire," she said, **"make for us a council fire."**

That worthy person spun on his heel and went to gather his equipment.

The chief looked straight at one of the clan. "**Wake the keeper of the night fire.**"

The clansman hurried away.

"**Healer,**" the chief said. The woman who was the senior healer came forward.

The chief spoke in a quieter tone. Gesturing at Daganu, who was still oblivious, she said, "**Seat him by the fire.**"

Last, she turned to the main body of the clan.

"**The council will meet,**" she said. "**Do not eat any of the mammoth. Not yet.**"

Councils did not exclude any member of the clan. Each was free to attend or not as suited their whim. Usually meetings were so deadly dull that the only clan people attending were those who must according to their responsibilities or those who had concerns which they wanted the council to address; however, this was to be no normal meeting. Everyone attended save for those whose responsibilities prevented them from doing so.

One whose responsibility precluded her attendance was the healer. She took Daganu by the arm and guided him to the day fire.

Daganu still showed no awareness of his surroundings. She had seen this before but only in cases of hunters who had been trampled or gored by dangerous prey during a hunt, and who had survived purely by great good luck. She had been told that this also could happen in the case of hunters returning from war with another clan or in cases of rape.

She did as she had been taught which is to say she sat quietly beside him and permitted him to come back to awareness on his own. Her task would not truly begin until that happened. Meanwhile she stayed close so he would not feel abandoned when his senses returned. It did not happen all at once. At first his empty gaze slowly regained focus. From staring at nothing as if blind he began to watch the fire. Muscles which had been taut began to relax. Slowly he looked around. His gaze reached the healer. His expression showed some confusion.

"Who are you?" he asked.

She replied, "**I am the healer.**"

He accepted that.

He scanned the surrounding area, expanding his sweep until it included the mountains across the valley. There were landmarks that he recognized. He looked back to the healer.

"You are Kakass Vag," he said.

It was the healer's turn to be unsure. "**I…do not know this name.**"

"I am Kakass. You are Kakass Vag. The people most like my people."

"**Oh,**" she said, comprehending.

He looked around again. "How did I get here?"

"**You came here through the forest. From over there.**"

"No. I was talking to chief. Now I am here. How?"

"**Oh! I see.**" The healer wondered what to say. "**Has this happened to you before?**"

"No. First time."

The healer thought for a moment. Then she had an idea. "**Did you speak your story before?**"

"No. No one to speak to."

"**Ah. That is magic of words. Speaking the words makes things feel more real. Real enough to strike you hard, and it feels like it all happens again.**"

Daganu considered this. It seemed to make sense. "I do not think I will speak of it again."

The keeper of the day fire had been tasked with building a council fire. There was, of course, a fire burning for all the uses a clan may have of it during the day. It cannot, however, meet the needs of a council fire. Council fires are unique; unlike a regular day or night fire, they are not intended to comfort or soothe. The spells spoken during the creation of a council fire are meant to promote alertness and clarity, and to compel truth.

The keeper of the night fire arrived as the spells were being cast. The keeper of the day fire, outranked, glanced at him. He was willing to step aside if his master wished it.

The keeper of the night fire had no such plan. His territory was the night. Daytime he left to his apprentice. He did, however, pay close attention to how the spells were cast. This focus caused the keeper of the day fire a certain degree of unease. Even the most competent can become nervous when performing tasks under the critical gaze of their superiors. The keeper of the night fire knew this well. It was a part of his duty as a teacher to cause this distress. An apprentice must be able to perform his duties flawlessly regardless of the stress he was under.

Besides, it was fun.

Once the council fire had been properly prepared, the elders settled down to discuss this utterly unprecedented event. They included the senior hunter, the cook, the tool maker, who also made weapons, both of the keepers of the fires, the tanner, the senior forager and the chief. Absent was the healer.

The chief drew a large breath. **"We speak before all the gods who will listen. Speak not with deceit, nor anger. A stranger has come among us, and we must decide what we will do."**

The senior forager asked, **"Has anyone heard of such a thing before?"**

It was the custom at council to address each other by title, not by name. The senior forager, however, was asking an open question to the entire council.

The tanner asked, **"Which part?"**

The senior hunter suggested, **"Let's begin with the monster that ate a clan."**

There was a general muttering of agreement.

"There have been clans that vanished."

"Usually in the winter. They have been thought to be lost to famine."

"What if they were eaten by a monster like this one?"

"This one bit a piece off a mountain!"

A general rumble of uneasiness travelled through the watchers from outside the council ring.

"Senior hunter, have you ever found a track from anything that could have been a monster like this?"

The senior hunter replied, **"I have been asking myself the same question. No. This thing must be bigger than a mammoth. I have found nothing like that."**

"Keeper of the night fire, are there stories of such things?"

"I think that question should be to the keeper of the lore."

The focus shifted to the chief, who answered, **"I know of no such story. But some day I will have to tell the story of this day. It will not be easy."**

"True. We do not know much about it. All we know is that it must be a monster."

"And we know that it must be enormous."

"That, at least, is something. Now we know there are giant monsters living in these mountains," said the chief.

Every councillor looked around the fire and each saw all the others shaking their heads in agreement.

"So, we move on to the stranger. We do not know how long he has been in our territory. It must have been for some time. Senior hunter, have you seen any tracks or signs that he was near here?"

In pride of rank the senior hunter answered, **"Not a thing. If he had made a track, I would have seen it. This man walks without disturbing the soil."**

Another nervous rumble came from the onlookers.

"What if the monster that ate the clan is following him?"

This time the onlookers did not murmur their unease. They roared their terror. Several fled the scene and dashed back to the shelter of their huts.

The chief rose and passed her steely gaze over the crowd. She did not speak; she did not need to. The respect she had earned from them ran so deep that the crowd quieted and slowly resumed their seats on the grass.

She returned to her seat. **"It is the stranger we must discuss,"** she said. **"What do we know of him?"**

"We know he is a mighty hunter."

"Your pardon, how do we know that?"

"He kills mammoths and longtooths. Alone!"

They all shook their heads in agreement.

The senior hunter mused, **"He would be a great asset in the hunt."**

"Do you mean we should take him into our clan?"

The chief interjected, **"It is forbidden."**

The senior forager looked puzzled. **"Do we not accept into our number young men and women from other clans?"**

"We do. But this hunter is not human."

"How do we know that?"

"He told us himself," said the chief.

"When? I missed it."

"He told us that all his clan are dead. Without a clan you are not human. We only accept humans into our clan."

The law was clear. No invitation would be given to the strange wandering hunter.

"So, what do we do? Just tell him he must go? He's dangerous."

"He must be driven out."

"We must take him by surprise."

"He must be soundly beaten so he does not return."

"What do we do with his spears?"

"We let him keep them. We are merciful."

"What of the longtooth necklace?"

"He also keeps the teeth. We do not know if he properly appeased the animal's spirit. We do not want a longtooth spirit coming after us seeking vengeance."

"What do we do with the mammoth meat?"

"That we keep."

There were general sounds of satisfaction. Some of the outlying clan members began to rise.

The chief called loudly, **"Not yet!"**

The people stopped uncertainly.

"We do not know if the monster is following him. After we drive the stranger out, we must leave this place. The monster may come here. Having come here, it might stay. When we leave, we must never come back, lest it begin to follow us. Once we leave we must make this valley taboo. And we must begin telling the story of this valley as a home to monsters and giants. We must protect our clan."

Beside the day fire Daganu and the healer sat. From time to time they heard a burst of noise from the direction of the council fire.

He had done all he could. He waited.

Eventually the Kakass Vag returned.

They walked to the day fire and encircled it.

The boys separated from the main group of men. They headed towards the huts. The older men came to stand close to Daganu. He thought they looked like hunters.

Daganu felt a surge of hope. He was a hunter. If he was to be accepted by the Kakass Vag, then this would be the group he joined.

The senior hunter made a signal.

The hunters descended upon Daganu. With fists they punched him. With feet they kicked him. Some grabbed pieces of firewood and used them as clubs.

The healer was as surprised as Daganu. She did not know what to do, but she recognized that this had been decided at the council, so she stood to one side and she watched.

As the beating continued the rest of the people shouted at him.

"You must leave!"
"You are not welcome!"
"You are not human!"
"Go away!"
"Take the monster with you!"
"Not human!"
"Not human!"

When he was near senseless they dragged him to the edge of the forest. Somebody dropped his spears beside him.

He looked up at them. Apparently the clan boys had run to fetch the spears for the hunters because they were now armed. They stood silently between Daganu and their clan.

Daganu got to his knees. He gathered his spears and used them to help himself stand. Slowly, with difficulty, he entered the forest. He did not look back. He moved down the slope because that was easier.

When he had vanished into the forest the hunters returned to the fires. The rest of the clan were already packing.

The hunters did not participate in the packing. They held their spears and stayed alert, watching the forest on all sides. Their role was protecting the clan. After all, there was a monster out there. And giants.

SEVEN

Daganu struggled down the slope. He hurt everywhere. The worst pain was the knowledge that the Kakass Vag had rejected him for the very reason he had gone to them.

He was not human.

He did know his body needed time to heal, and for that he must find a safe place to rest. Or he could give up and just die. That would not be difficult to achieve. He need only stop trying.

No.

That simply was not part of him.

He was a long way down into the valley. He stopped and sat on a fallen log. He could not go much further. He sat there in what was late morning sunlight. It was hard to believe that so much could happen in so short a time. Yesterday he had hope. At dawn today he had hope.

Right now…now was not a good time.

Oh, he hurt. How could he hunt when he was in this damaged state?

For lack of anything better to do he looked around. He recognized an edible plant. Wait, there were two kinds, and there seemed to be a good growth of them. At least he would not starve. Not for a while. Oh, a third type of food plant. He silently thanked the head forager who had trained him in the use of plants.

It had long ago been recognized that foraging for plants was the core of survival. You lost some strength without meat, but it was plant lore that kept a clan alive. Plants were much more reliable as a food source than meat. This was why the clan did both. Food plants kept you alive. Meat made you strong.

Sitting in the sun made him feel somewhat better, but he felt tired.

Daganu had always thought that the bone-deep weariness that accompanies serious injury was unfair. When you are injured or sick, that was the time when you would feel weakest. It was also when you needed to be strongest. If he had made the world, it would not be so. It was a shame the gods had not asked for his guidance.

He found a nice sunlit place where he could lay. He curled up in nest of grass and fell asleep.

It was probably the pain that woke him. While it is true that you heal best by sleeping, it is also true that your fresh injuries stiffen up. Daganu could barely move.

The sun was no longer shining on the place where he lay.

He stood up with a mighty effort. He deeded to drink. He looked around, reading the lay of the land. Water would most likely be…that way.

Slow steps took him in that direction. He stopped frequently to regain some measure of strength, but in due course he did find several old mammoth tracks. They were holding water. Now all he needed to do was to get low enough to reach it.

He accomplished this by the simplest and most reliable method that existed: he fell down. He stifled a shout of agony. There was no point in broadcasting his sorry state to any predators or scavengers in the vicinity. After a rest he quenched his thirst.

Oh, that was good.

He looked around. In normal circumstances, he would not have dreamed of remaining beside a water source. All meat eaters know that if you watch a water hole, prey will come.

He could only think of two exceptions to the rule: one was a river. The full length of the river bank was a water source, and it was found on both sides of the river. There was just too much ground to watch. The other exception was a water source that normally was not a water source. A mammoth track fit into that category quite nicely.

Daganu rested. He did not sleep much because of the pain, but rest is often enough. He built a fire. It took longer than it should have.

"I move like Huth," he thought to himself.

He considered that. The oldest hunter was in pain most of the time. Huth was an object of curiosity to the children. He moved the slowest, and he moved differently from all the other adults.

Old Simfa was the elder who spoke most often of why the things are as they are, but she was not the only one.

One warm night when the clan was gathered around the fire, Bossa, a girl child, asked Huth a question. "Why do you walk so strange?"

Warm nights were the favourite times for the clan. Most adults had no actual schedule for their activities, so through the daylight times it seemed that a few or many of them were always apart from the main group. Evenings were when the clan gathered around the fire. It was the social centre of the Kakass. If it was warm they were at their most comfortable and most relaxed.

The child had addressed a question to Huth. It must be answered. Huth smiled. The clan was a big, happy extended family. For most of the time they got along well with each other, and all enjoyed interacting with the children.

"I am old," Huth replied, "but once I was as young as you are."

The child looked sceptical.

"Nobody begins old. We all start out as babies, just as you did. As the seasons pass you get older. You do know that someday you will be a grown-up woman, don't you?"

Bossa shook her head yes. As with all children through time, growing up was eagerly anticipated.

"Even after you are grown up, the seasons still pass. You get older. After many seasons you get old.

"That is no mystery. It just takes a long time."

Bossa shook her head doubtfully. "But why do you walk so strange?"

"Many, many seasons have passed for me. I have been hurt many times. When you are hurt you do not always heal well. Hurts to my legs that didn't heal properly add up and the pain makes me limp. I limp with both legs because all *of my old hurts. Pain in my back makes my limp worse. I suppose that is why I walk strangely. My arms and my hands hurt all of the time as well."*

Bassa went over to Huth and gave him a hug. Matter of factly she said, "When I grow up, I will fix you."

Huth smiled, and hugged her in return.

Daganu now began to understand Huth a little better. Huth had often said that sitting in the warm sun or close to the fire helped to reduce the aching. Daganu added wood to the fire.

The night was cold. It passed very slowly.

Daganu was young and strong. Young, strong people heal fast. Sunrise found him somewhat better. He still hurt all over, but movement was easier.

He had another drink and stood up. He needed food. He began walking back to where he had seen all the edibles. Even though he walked slowly, he arrived sooner than he expected. He had remembered the distance being much farther.

The next few days fell into a simple routine of eating, drinking, and resting. It wasn't long before that routine proved unsatisfying. He must decide what to do next. He would continue to seek a way to regain his humanity. That was beyond question.

What had gone wrong with the Kakass Vag?

He remembered the repeated shout that he was not human. It was what he would have expected from the Kakass if he had been banished and tried to return. He had chosen the Kakass Vag for his first attempt because they were so much like his clan. It seemed that a better choice would be a people somewhat less like his.

There was an obvious choice. He shied away from it because it was distasteful to him. Still, as much as he tried to find an alternative his mind kept returning to them.

The tales of the Kakass identified caves as entrances into the Earth Mother. To enter a cave was to enter the flesh of the Earth Mother. The flesh of the Earth Mother is foundation of all life and is to be treated with the proper respect. Some ceremonies were best done within a cave, but they were not for casual use. Daganu had found several cave entrances. He had never gone inside. He had not had the pressing need to do so, and respect for the Earth Mother barred his way.

But there was a clan that lived in caves. To the Kakass, this act was sacrilege. Caves were held to be holy. Taking shelter in a cave when conditions made it necessary was acceptable. The Earth Mother cared about people, but only people who deserved to be cared for. To eat, argue, fart and everything else associated with living and to do it on a daily basis inside a cave, well, that was evil.

But was it worse than being non-human?

By the fire one evening he realized that he had been looking at the flames without noticing them. This is not uncommon; however, to stare unseeing for long periods of time is. The sun had been setting, or at least that was the last thing he remembered. He had just fed the fire. Now it was near full dark, and the fire was shrinking to coals and ash.

I should feed the fire, he thought.

He did not move.

As the darkness deepened around him, he watched the fire die. The coals grew dimmer, and the ash became thicker.

Still he did not move. Eventually he saw no signs of life in the fire.

He knew that he should now move into his shelter. It seemed so far away. He continued to sit. There were things to do, but he just didn't care.

He woke in the morning coved with dew beside the cold ashes. Physically he was not at all happy, but emotionally he felt somewhat better. At least he would be able to move and seek some answers to the worst of his problems. He didn't let himself dwell on how likely it was that he could find them.

In a few more days Daganu had healed enough that he felt able to cross mountain passes. He certainly did not want to stay in this valley. He decided to backtrack to the nightward and again cross the pass that had brought him here. Once across the pass he would follow the river of the valley beyond toward downstream. That would take him to the right of sunrise.

He had no idea what he would find that direction, but at this time that sounded like a fine thing. Careful planning had done him no good. It was time to put his trust in the gods. Hopefully they would guide him well.

He had been relieved of the basket full of smoked mammoth by the Kakass Vag so the load he was carrying was much lighter. One might expect him to travel faster unburdened, but such was not the case. His travels before had a specific goal. Now he was just wandering and healing.

Some days he felt energy and strode as if with a purpose. More often he wandered slowly and aimlessly.

The season had advanced. Daganu had healed fully and some berries were now ripe. These were eagerly sought by the people and fully enjoyed. Much time was spent contentedly picking and eating the juicy morsels. One needed to be alert in a berry patch. Bears, wolves and foxes liked to eat berries as well. Foxes were no threat but the others needed to be treated with caution.

Daganu was in a berry patch when he noticed something. Most of the berries had already been picked. That was not unusual, but it occurred to him that the berry bushes were in better condition than they should be. Bears especially have a habit of stripping off and gulping down everything on a branch including the leaves and smaller branches. Wolves and foxes are less destructive but eat far fewer berries. It can be difficult to see that they have been there at all.

This berry patch had clearly been harvested but most of the leaves remained on the branch tips. That was a strong indicator that it had been people who had been here before Daganu arrived. Now that he had been alerted, Daganu could read other signs as well.

Grass had been flattened showing a trail through the patch. Bears left this type of sign as well, but their trails had a different appearance and tended to move through a berry patch randomly. These trails were nearly in a straight line. There were also parallel trails that did not cross each other. People had definitely been here sometime in the last few days.

The overwhelming question was this: who were the people picking berries in this area? Another vital question was: what should he do?

He really had only two choices. The first was to leave now, flee, and trust that no one would follow, and the second was to find out who the unknown foragers were and to take some action based on what he learned.

That's not really much of a choice. Daganu always wanted to know things. If he didn't like the answers he got that was simply too bad. So was there a safe way to learn what he needed to know?

He was a hunter. He would follow the sign he had until he tracked the people to their lair. When he lost the trail, as was normal, he would very carefully continue to travel in the direction the tracks had been leading. If he found more sign by doing this, then that would be good. If not, he would be return to the point where he had lost the trail. From there he would move in careful circles until he found more sign that he could track.

However, in this case he tried an unreliable technique. He studied the nearby terrain and guessed which way the foragers had gone. He then travelled some distance in that direction in the hopes that he would find new tracks. The benefit of this was that tracking can be very slow. Jumping ahead could save him a great deal of time; but if he was wrong, he could lose even more time.

He did not find the trail where he expected it to be.

Perhaps he would see campfire smoke as he had in the case of the Kakass Vag. However he found them, and find them he would, he would stay a decent distance away from them until he had learned all that he needed to know. He did not want to repeat his experiences with the Kakass Vag. The bruises had healed, but his confidence had not.

A good hunter knows the habits of his quarry. People in his experience were divided into two main groups; hunters and foragers. The berry patch had been visited by a group of pickers. Hunters would have eaten a snack and moved on. This patch had been picked by people trying to harvest everything. This evidence meant the pickers must have been foragers.

If it had been hunters there would have been no telling how distant from the main encampment they had been. Hunters could be several valleys away from the main camp and berries were difficult to carry without baskets. Baskets were not standard equipment for hunters. If the hunt was successful the hunters would make new baskets to carry the meat, just as Daganu had when he scavenged the mammoth meat.

Foragers would not have been far from the camp. It would definitely be in this valley and probably even on this side of the valley.

That seemed doable.

He moved up the slope to reach the higher meadows favoured by clans like the Kakass. They were empty. Not only that but they held some excellent berry patches which were heavy with fruit. If this obvious bounty was untouched but further down the slope the patches had been harvested it would seem that the camp must be much lower on the slope.

That was unusual.

Oh, well, all that meant was that these people had some different habits than those he was used to. He must take his search lower.

Different habits…perhaps these people didn't know what makes a person human. One can always hope.

He made his way down to the river and cautiously walked the forest edge nearest the riverbank. He chose to search moving upstream because going that direction the valley would eventually end. Follow a river downstream and you will find yourself travelling a long way. River would join river and the combined flow would be larger. Follow it far enough and…no one knew where rivers really went. They travelled further than any of the people he had knowledge of.

As it turned out, upstream was the correct choice. He had not travelled far when he found the tracks of some people. The feet that made them were smaller than Daganu's. That suggested that they had been made by women.

After he had followed them for a while the tracks became a trail. Whoever it was had been staying here for a while. The trail became more distinct and soon enough joined with another trail. After that the trail became so well used that the grasses had been worn away creating a trail of packed dirt.

Daganu had become nervous. Who stayed in one place so long that they wore away the grass on the trails?

He had been on high alert for so long that he needed to rest. Concentration saps your energy in a way similar to physical exertion. He stepped away from the trail carefully so he left little or no sign of his passing. He looked for and found a sun dappled spot that was dry and comfortable. Here he would stay until he had puzzled through what he had found. It would also be his chance to rest.

The sun moved across the sky. Daganu was no closer to solving the riddle of the paths. Then he heard the sound of voices.

As these voices neared, he could tell that it was women who were walking on the path. This must be a group of foragers. At this time of day, it was probable that they were returning to their camp.

He allowed them to go well past before he set foot upon the path again. He would follow this group. No matter where they were going, he would learn something. He followed at such a distance that he occasionally caught a glimpse of them. They were carrying baskets. It was another indication of foragers.

Foragers heading home seldom look behind themselves. Even hunters do not look at their back trail much. He felt quite safe following, especially because he maintained a healthy distance from them.

What caused him some concern was the fact that they seemed to be going in a direction that made no sense.

He had viewed the valley quite thoroughly from the high meadows. There were no clearings near here. Any huts built here would be in the forest with no open view.

Predators or enemy clan war parties could approach in secret. Yet he could begin to smell wood smoke.

The path was headed toward a cliff. He supposed building your camp with a cliff to its back did make some sense. It would make the camp more defendable. It would not, however, have been his choice.

He caught one final glimpse of the foraging party. It nearly made him gasp.

They were walking into an opening in the rock of the cliff itself.

He had found a clan of Live In The Grounds.

He immediately turned about and headed back along the trail. He needed to find some sanctuary where he could come to terms with this. Only then could he decide what to do.

He moved with extreme care. He wanted to leave no trace of his passage, and to give that strange clan no warning of his presence. If he was to make contact, he wanted it to be by his choice alone.

By reflex Daganu went upslope. The Kakass preferred to camp partway up a slope and in a clearing. It was difficult for an enemy to sneak up unseen and it was away from the worst of the biting insects. On a hot day you could be in a cooling breeze. Besides, there was a view.

Winters were different. The same wind that felt so good during the summer instead would chill you to the bone. Biting insects were not an issue. Enemies rarely were a threat. Travel in the winter snows was difficult. Enemies remained in their own territory.

As a result, Daganu soon found himself on the lower edge of a mountainside clearing. He stopped just short of the grass. This was a case where it would be best to remain out of view.

For a while, he simply stood where he was.

Live In The Grounds. He had never actually expected to find some. They were not common. Or at least, that was what he had believed.

He was beginning to question the truth of some of the things that he had always believed. He had believed that his clan would be there for him forever. He was wrong. He had believed that the Kakass Vag would welcome him if he ever met them. He was wrong. He had believed that the mountains were solid, reliable and unchanging. He was wrong, wrong and wrong.

He realized that he was curled up in a ball on the ground beneath a spruce tree. I should get up, he thought.

But when darkness had taken the land he was still there.

The morning dew left him damp and chilled. He had slept past sunrise. There were no clouds in the sky. Feeling more like himself, Daganu arose. It did not take long for him to find a location that was both hidden from the lower elevations and open to the newly risen sun. This area was where he would face the day.

Finding a suitably hidden spot, he started a fire. Fires have many uses. They cook the meat and warm the chilled clansman. They provide light in the dark and were the path through which there could be communication with the gods. This was a comfort fire. Where a fire was became a camp. Lacking any permanent home, a camp was as strong an anchor point as the Kakass ever had. It was security.

Having created as secure a place as possible, Daganu was now able to finally consider what he should do next.

A cave is an entrance into the very flesh of the Earth Mother, and it is a holy place. Thus went the teachings that all Kakass children learned. To live in a cave is to defile it. Any may enter a cave, but it must be done with the proper reverence.

Spending a night in a cave is acceptable if you are sheltering from a storm, an attack from a rival clan or the like. A Live In The Ground clan treats a cave as if it was a hut. It is clearly unacceptable.

And yet…

If he somehow managed to join the Live In The Ground clan, he would not be alone any more. He could reclaim his humanity. The temptation was huge.

The attempt to join the Kakass Vag had failed because they were too similar to the Kakass in their beliefs and therefore they were unwilling to take in a non-human. The Live In The Ground beliefs were clearly not the same. Who could say how they might react? They might not even realize that Daganu was not human any longer. That would open the option of him joining them.

But, what they were doing was so wrong.

Perhaps they could be taught to live properly. He could teach them the truth. That could work. That would solve all the problems quite neatly.

By this time Daganu had been contemplating the issues for a long time. The day was spent. He could make his attempt tomorrow. For tonight he would sleep unsheltered.

EIGHT

Morning came and Daganu, the unlikeliest of missionaries, stood with his eyes closed, searching for courage.

When he had walked into the Kakass Vag encampment he had been carrying a basket of mammoth meat as a gift. While the gift had not been enough to sway the council, it might have bought him some time.

For the Live In The Grounds he had nothing.

He stood just out of sight of the cave entrance. He was trying to come up with some sort of plan for winning favour. Nothing came to mind. This lack of inspiration made the chance of being accepted less than it could be. He decided to observe the cave for a while longer. Something might happen to give him that inspiration.

He sat in a patch of shrubs some distance from the cave. He could see the cave mouth clearly and a portion of the path that led to, or from, it. From this far away he could see no details on the figures that moved in and out.

They spent most of their time within the cave. To Daganu it seemed they had no respect for the Earth

Mother. How they failed to realize their blunder was beyond him. Even more mystifying was the fact that the Earth Mother had yet to punish them for violating her. Perhaps she was waiting for Daganu to correct them for her.

Days had passed and he had learned very little. There seemed to be no pattern to the comings and goings of hunters or foragers. Daganu had a large store of patience, but it was beginning to run thin. If the Earth Mother did wish for him to teach the ways of respect to the Live In The Grounds, perhaps he should get the job done.

Just do it. As with the story of what caves are for, as with beginning the search for the Kakass Vag, his mantra seemed to fit the situation. Just do it. Drawing in a huge breath, he walked around the final screen of bush, listening for shouts of recognition. Or anger.

The morning remained quiet.

He advanced to the edge of spear throwing range, stopped and he stood.

And he stood.

Sooner or later, he thought, somebody will see me.

He squatted on the trail with both spears in one hand, their butts firmly planted on the soil, trying to show confidence but no threat.

"Stranger!" someone shouted from within.

There was a sound of people bustling about, and armed hunters rushed out to defend home and kin, for all the world like an ant hill you had poked with a stick.

Daganu remained in his squat.

The hunters stood firmly between the intruder and the cave, all grasping their heavy thrusting spears. Their furs were worn in the same manner as a Kakass would, but their faces were tattooed. Daganu had never seen that before.

Daganu rose slowly to his feet. "Hello," he said.

"What did he say?" one of the hunters asked.

He had asked the hunter standing next to him. This one appeared to be the senior hunter. *"Don't ask me!"* the senior hunter replied unhelpfully.

"Keep an eye open for more of them," he added.

Daganu could not understand them. Whereas the Kakass Vag had pronounced their words differently than he did, these people used different words entirely. He suddenly doubted that they would be able to communicate much of anything. Coming here at all now seemed to be a very bad idea.

"Does anyone here understand what I am saying?" he asked.

"What should we do?"
"Where do you suppose he came from?"
"We should catch him."

There was a murmur of general agreement to this last statement. Live In The Ground people were accustomed to other clans treating them with hostility; as a result they were quicker than most to reach for their own weapons.

From the direction of the cave came a woman's voice. *"Get rid of it!"*

Daganu saw the subtle shift in posture that hunters tended to make just before attacking. He also saw several of the Live In The Ground hunters change their grips on their spears.

He turned and ran like a rabbit. Two hunters threw their spears at him, but they were thrusting spears and they were not balanced for throwing. They missed.

With shouts most of the hunters set off in pursuit. A few stayed behind to continue to protect their clan.

"Be careful! It could be a trap!" shouted one of those who remained.

This shouted warning had the effect of slowing the pursuing band, if only by a fraction. It wasn't much, but every bit counts when you are fleeing for your life.

Daganu leaped sideways off the trail to run through a patch of prickly shrubs. He didn't even notice the scratches he sustained, but his pursuers noticed theirs. Daganu gained more ground.

Daganu scanned the terrain ahead for anything he could use to delay the hunter group. He saw a wasp nest in a small tree. He shifted his course to pass directly beneath it. As he passed the tree he struck the tree hard with his open hand.

The wasps, of course, were highly offended.

Wasps in daylight always have some sentries on duty outside the nest. These chased Daganu. The bulk of the wasp army is normally inside the nest. It takes time for them to come swarming out looking for something to battle. Daganu was beyond their view before this happened.

But his pursuers were just entering their view. It was not good timing on their part. While Daganu was stung twice, the hunter group pursuing him fared considerably worse.

The hunters retreated. This was effectively the end of the chase.

Some time, and it felt like a long time, after he had made it to the other side or the river, Daganu stopped to recover his breath. He did not believe he was finished running. If it had been the Kakass camp and *he* had driven a stranger away he would not simply dismiss him as gone for good.

Someone would be on his trail, and very soon.

True, the Kakass Vag did not pursue him. However, that was a very different situation. They had let him go. Indeed, they watched him walk away.

This state of affairs, in contrast, had been an attack failed and a pursuit foiled. That was two failures. Pride had been injured. They would certainly make another attempt to kill him.

In the meantime, Daganu did not enjoy being stung. He looked about seeking one of the most respected plants, which he knew as stingweed. It had leaves which were divided into many small threadlike leaflets and it had flowers that were white and grew in nearly flat-topped clusters. This part was what he picked when he found the stingweed. He chewed the flowers until they were in a coarse paste, and this he put onto the sting sites as a poultice. In a short time the poultice had done an admirable job. The stings had nearly stopped the hurting. The same plant could stop the itching cause by biting insects. That was actually the most common use of the plant.

Feeling better, Daganu looked at the sky. The very best thing that could happen for him was that a heavy rain would wash the traces of his passage away. The signs he could read in the sky promised several days of beautiful clear weather. It seemed that the sky god was not his friend today.

Very well, does the river god like him any better?

The river god is a jealous god and it is never satisfied. It is continually making changes to the riverbed. It places uprooted trees here and there as decorations. These dead trees in turn make eddies that both grow and fade, and they dig new depressions. But nothing else is permitted to leave its mark. Tracks do not last long here, nor do constructions such as fish weirs. By now the crude dams Daganu had made to aid him catching fish would by now be vanished without a trace.

If Daganu was to walk in the river, especially where the current was strong, his tracks would be gone long before nightfall.

There were two problems with this. The first problem was that this was water from the glaciers, and it was extremely cold. Before long Daganu's feet would lose sensation and his balance would be compromised.

The second problem, and the one that worried Daganu more, was that in order to use the river to hide his tracks he would need to spend considerable time out in the open. There was no place in the valley that he would be more obvious.

A decision had to be made. His pursuers would have returned to the cave to gather supplies and throwing spears for a long chase. That would not take much time. If he did not act soon, it would be too late.

He stepped into the water. It was very cold. In his race to escape his pursuers he had ended up somewhat downstream of where the Live In The Grounds lived. He had no desire to move any closer to their cave, which made his choice of direction easy. He began to walk further downstream.

He would spend as much time in the water as he was capable of tolerating. The icy water numbed his feet, but only after going through a period of serious pain. Eventually the pain would recede and they would be as sensitive as blocks of wood. This was when Daganu learned that numb feet were a hazard as well. If your feet are numb, it becomes very easy to trip over things or kick obstacles beneath the surface. The fourth toe on his left foot had encountered a rock and was turning completely black. He thought it was probably broken.

He would not be able to run much for a while, but he no longer believed that the Live In The Ground hunters could follow him, even if they had the determination to hunt him down.

He had travelled a considerable distance. He left the river at a place where he could reach the forest by walking exclusively on bare rock. As soon as the water dried there would be no trace of him passing. Daganu doubted that he would be able to follow his own tracks. If the Live In The Grounds somehow tracked him this far they would have no way of knowing where he had exited the water.

As for his own hunt, he had run out of ideas. For now, he would simply focus on survival. His injured toe made it very difficult to move with the stealth he could usually manage.

He watched for ravens circling and listened for them arguing.

After a time, he did hear ravens. He limped toward their racket, trusting them to lead him to the remains of a kill made by other, uninjured predators.

He really liked birds.

When ravens led him to the remains of a great deer he surveyed the situation. The scavengers had been here for a while and the amount of meat remaining on the skeleton was pathetic.

No matter. He was able to wrest two upper leg bones from the skeleton. These would suffice. After successfully scavenging the bones he moved far from the kill site. Such places were seriously unsafe.

In a safe place he found a good hammer stone. A nearby boulder served as an anvil. Rotating the bone, he struck it numerous times.

Inexperienced hunters often made the mistake of striking too hard. There is nothing to be gained in breaking the bone with one mighty blow. Fragments would fly away carrying with them much of the contents hidden within.

Long bones are hollow. They hold treasure.

The bone Daganu was working accumulated many tiny fractures in a ring encircling the shaft. When he judged these were sufficient he lifted the bone by one end and brought it sharply down upon the boulder. It broke very nicely at the point where Daganu had been working. Inside the hollow of the long bones you can find marrow. It is soft, fatty, high protein and utterly delicious. It is such a rich food source that you do not need much in order to have a good meal. Daganu loved it both raw and cooked.

He saved the second bone for a cooked meal in the evening.

Some days later a small group of hunters were ready to set out. One of them was a youth on his first real hunting trip. He was very excited. Your first hunting trip was a passage from childhood to adulthood. He had been presented with two spears by the chief and blessed by the keeper of the night fire. Mackesh, the hunt leader, had solemnly quizzed him of his duties.

"You must be alert at all times. What is your first concern?"

"I must always know what direction we are travelling and where we are. We must always be able to find the main camp."

"Good. On this hunt we begin by travelling slightly to the right of sunward, almost directly to where the sun rose this morning. So what direction do we expect to travel on the way back?"

"We would travel slightly to the right of nightward, where the sun sets in the evening."

"Yes. Keep in mind which of the two directions we are headed. What other things must you do?"

"I must watch for danger, for animals and for signs of animals."

"Sign of animals are…?"

"Tracks, broken or bent plants, movements in the trees or tall grasses, and the smells and sounds of other animals."

"Are you ready to put yourself at risk to provide for the clan?"

"Yes!" exclaimed the youth fervently. The watching clan chuckled.

"You had a name before. It is now forgotten. Today you become Sutt."

The newly named Sutt knew he would remember this hunting trip for the rest of his life. He had no idea that the other hunters would also remember it for the rest of their days.

Ceremonies completed, Mackesh turned with no more words and led the hunting party out of the camp.

Daganu did not move far in a day because his toe pained him greatly; however, he made a point of crossing a pass into another valley. Although he had evaded his pursuers, he had no faith in the idea that the Live In The Grounds had given up. He travelled when he felt that he could, and kept moving through two more valleys, then three valleys.

Finally satisfied, he found himself in a place where there were abundant water sources and plentiful food plants. His broken toe had been abused during his flight from the valley of the cave. The constant flexing of the toe had prevented any healing. Here he could rest and begin to recover.

It was just as well. He was very tired, both physically and emotionally.

He was no longer certain that he would ever find a group that did not attack him. The Kakass Vag were very similar to his own people, but they had cast him out. Live In The Grounds were very unlike the Kakass, and they had tried to kill him. What was left?

Perhaps it was time to accept that he was an animal and resign himself to remaining as one. Although he knew no stories about an exile living out his life as an animal, it was possible that his future was on that path.

Whatever. Daganu found a sheltered place in some shrubs and went to sleep.

The hunting party moved in what appeared to be a haphazard manner, yet they travelled quite a distance the first day. They did not do much hunting. They were searching for meat to take home to their clan; something big enough or numerous enough to be worth ending the hunt. Also, this was Sutt's first hunt. It was incumbent upon the other hunters that he was given a memorable hunt.

A set of sheep tracks had brought them from a mineral lick in the low areas to the high meadows.

As they crossed one meadow, a hunter named Ballapak paused. He looked one way and then the other. Then he pursed his lips and made a squeaking sound.

The squeak caught the attention of his clansmen and they stopped. When he was satisfied that they were watching, he pointed to the ground at his feet. Then he pointed to the grass where he was standing and slowly lifted his hand until he pointed to the trees at the edge of the clearing.

The message was clear. Something had travelled through here and had gone that way.

The group gathered together to investigate the signs. Standing close together they could talk in soft voices without fear of alerting game or enemy of their presence. Still, they spoke little.

"No hoof marks. Soft feet."

"People?"

"Looks like it to me."

"Not old."

Mackesh stood and scanned the middle distances. In muddy ground or loose, dry soil the tracks are clearest when you look down not far from your own feet. In grass, however, it is easier to pick out where something has gone at some distance from you. The shine of the grass changes where something had bent it over. You can even tell what direction it had travelled.

Mackesh felt no more need of conversation. He simply began to walk, following the trail.

When they entered the wooded area, another tracking method was used. Fallen leaves or spruce needles were darker where they had been disturbed. Here the trackers switched back and forth between looking to the distance and to the ground at their feet. The leaves on the forest floor are drier on the top, moister on the underside.

When an experienced tracker is on such a trail, he can follow at a surprising pace, and they were all experienced trackers, even Sutt. He had spent large parts of many days practising near the camp, as all prospective hunters do.

It was not a very long time before they were gathered around the dead ashes of a campfire.

"I only see sign for one person," said Mackesh, the leader.

"Me too."

"Did we have anyone scouting out this way?"

"I don't think so."

"What clan would come onto our land?"

"I can't think of any."

"We need to find out."

"Agreed."

They began to look for the signs which would tell them which way the mystery person had gone.

For the first time in a long while Daganu felt relaxed.

His long-term goal remained the same but thanks to his injury the urgency had declined. If something simply cannot be done, then let it rest. You can always start again when the conditions are right.

For now, his priority was to rest and heal.

Lately he was using his digging stick far more than his spears. Plants don't need to be chased much. As any hunter does, he preferred to eat meat, not only for its flavour but also because it was a higher status food.

Empty pride is not a good enough reason to starve.

He normally tended to travel through the higher mountain meadows for the views they afforded. A high vantage increased the odds of him seeing a campfire smoke. To be truthful, an equal reason was that he simply enjoyed the views.

Another, newer, reason to stay high was that the Live In The Ground band he had encountered lived near the bottom of their valley. He did not know if this was true of all such ground-living bands but he was guided by what little experience he had. So, he kept as much as he could to the higher elevations.

When he sat in his camps, he always tried to do something useful, something that would aid him when he was able to return to his quest. If he returned to his quest. For now, that was braiding more cord from grasses. As a result his supply of cord was large. As he looked at it he smiled. He could go hunting after all.

In the high mountain meadows, you can find marmots. In recent years any marmots he had killed were cases of opportunity and a good throw with spear or stone. Spending any larger amount of time pursuing this small game did not seem reasonable when he always had a destination or was looking for big game.

He had plenty of time now. He would go snaring marmots which was a method if hunting he had rarely done since childhood. The idea was strangely appealing. He began looking through his coils of cord, looking for a length appropriate to his needs.

This was going to be fun.

The hunter group were moving slowly, but they had found the ashes of another campfire.

"This isn't far from the first camp," one mused.

"Not far at all."

"That's strange."

"Not a trader, then. Traders like to move faster than this guy."

"It's not right for a scout, either. What is he doing?"

"I'm not complaining. He barely leaves any sign. If he was moving farther and faster, we would never track him down."

There were sounds of general agreement.

"Sutt," said the leader. **"Go back to camp and let them know what we are doing. I have no idea how long this will take."**

Sutt was young and eager. He had not been travelling with the main hunting group for long and this was the first time he had been sent out on a solo task more than a day's travel from the main camp. He shook his head in agreement and promptly set out. He jogged.

The leader smiled. He remembered being that eager to prove himself.

Then his gaze returned to the campfire ash. The ash did not speak to him. There were so many things he wanted to know.

"So, stranger, what are you doing?"

Daganu was lying in the grass waiting for the marmot to stick its head out of the hole.

It was pleasant to be quietly lying in the sun on a warm summer day while around him were many marmots of the same opinion. They were watching him, more out of habit than any feeling of threat. He was too far away from them to pose any hazard if he should run toward them, and he had shown no ability to fly. So, they sunbathed with the certainty that he was no threat.

They were not entirely correct.

Come on, friend marmot. Won't you join me for dinner?

Of course he said nothing aloud.

The sun is shining.

The day is warm.

The grass is juicy.

I mean you harm.

Now, friend marmot, how can you resist that?

It seemed that the marmot could resist it quite well. Daganu was comfortable enough that he was getting sleepy. Hunting can be hard work.

All right, it wasn't in this case, but it can be. Really.

Daganu's mind was wandering all over the place. He sternly told himself to concentrate. This hunt was his only reasonable chance to eat meat today.

Ravens suddenly began chattering excitedly. They make a guttural croak much of the time and that is generally known as the sound of a raven, but in truth they have a large vocabulary. If you spend the time and effort, you can learn a lot of it and extract some information from it.

These ravens had just witnessed a kill.

What they had not told Daganu was what kind of predator had done the killing. *That* mattered. If it was a longtooth, Daganu wanted no part of it. A pack of wolves would leave nothing for a hungry ex-human. But if it was a bear…that was the point where things became interesting.

A bear probably would leave enough to be worth scavenging, and it would move off to sleep after it had dined, but if it happened to return while Daganu was taking his cut, Daganu would be risking death. That… would be a challenge, especially with an injured foot. It would be just like the situation the longtooth had been in.

He considered how likely it was that the kill, whatever it was, would be accessible to him. This was the moment chosen by the marmot to stick his head out of the hole. Reflexively Daganu pulled the snare tight onto the rodent's neck.

The decision had been made: a marmot on a string was worth more than a bear in the bush.

By day's end he had three dead marmots - a credible total. Gut them up here, cook one before dark, and he would have the next day's rations as well. He would be able to begin travelling at his slow pace any time he pleased. It had been a good day, indeed.

It had been a frustrating, disgusting day, thought Mackesh. This intruder wasn't doing anything right. Apart from not leaving enough sign to easily follow, which slowed his group to what felt like a crawl, he insisted on spending most of his time in the high meadows. What was that about? His clan were lowlanders and forest dwelling people.

In order to track something or someone well you needed to understand your quarry's habits. The only habit Mackesh had identified was this infatuation with high places, something he definitely did not share.

"Enough," he said. *"We make camp here."*

"What about shelter?"

"We will sleep rough, under the open sky. There is no rain on the wind."

You can smell rain coming most of the time.

There was no debate. Mackesh had not asked for the job of leader. He did not want it. But the others had recognized his talents and automatically looked to him for guidance. He read all types of sign better than the others and he thought well. He often could make sense of what his fellows saw to be confusion. And he never panicked. That is no small thing.

Ballapak began making the fire. Choosing an appropriate site was a skill they all shared. A fire was necessary. Even if the heat was not required and there would be no cooking, both true this day, flame was the connection to the gods. It would be best to keep the lines of communication open.

Mackesh could not think of an appropriate question for the gods. Still, the fire must be ready in case of emergency. It was better to be able to call upon the gods at a moment's notice than to be unable to if in need.

The group sat around the fire eating jerky. No one felt like talking.

NINE

Daganu sat on the edge of a precipice with his feet dangling over the edge. As he idly picked at a sliver he had somehow picked up, he pondered the situation. One of the drawbacks of trying to travel by way of high meadows was encountering barriers like this. A small river had cut a sheer-walled canyon across his direction of travel. He had no dislike of such things. Indeed, he had benefitted from a similar canyon not long ago.

He stroked the longtooth necklace as he studied the barrier.

His injury would make things more difficult. A possible route down this side and up the other he reluctantly rejected because he could not trust his left foot as much as he would need to. He would have to move either uphill or down in order to find an easier crossing.

It's just as well, he thought, that he was in no hurry.

At Daganu's most recent camp Mackesh read the signs. He ran a finger gently through the ashes. Fragile ash formations crumbled. There had been some strong gusts of wind yesterday. This ash could not have survived them.

"This is last night's fire," he announced. *"We are close."*

"He has been eating marmot."

"That's easy prey up here." Mackesh began thinking aloud. *"He has been moving slowly and hunting only small, easy game. Do you suppose he is ill or hurt?"*

"That would fit. I think you're right."

"I still have no idea why he is here," complained Mackesh. *"I hate not knowing."*

"So, let's catch him and find out."

They resumed tracking the stranger, sending one hunter circling ahead to try to find his trail. If this could be done it would save a significant amount of time. They had been trying this for a while without success. But this time the forward patrol found a clear track.

It seemed the gods were finally smiling upon them.

The gods must be cursing him. That was what Daganu thought. After moving steadily for so long, he was completely stymied. Every place he had looked at the chasm it had been impassable. Malignant forces must be at work.

Tension can be as tiring as hard work. Daganu was exhausted. It couldn't possibly hurt to rest for a while. He found a cozy depression with a good growth of grass to act as a mattress. It was protected from the wind if it should rise. Soon he was asleep.

"Mackesh!" the front hunter hissed. *"Look at this."*

Some grass had clearly been trodden on. The unusual thing was that it appeared to be slowly rebounding to its pre-trodden state.

Getting close to the hunter Mackesh softly murmured, *"Very fresh."*

Looking back at the rest of the group he signalled for them to move up and to split into two groups. These he sent ahead, one group to the left and the other to the right.

He allowed them to advance ahead of where he stood.

He could see the edge of the canyon that had stopped Daganu. Feeling that events were reaching a conclusion he signalled every hunter to draw together. They were closing in on where the sign indicated the intruder would be.

Daganu woke suddenly. When he looked around, he saw unknown hunters. His experience with such people had been anything but good.

His instinctive response was to leap to his feet and sprint away!

He did leap to his feet but his injured foot collapsed beneath him and he sprawled face first to the ground. Before he had the chance to rise again one of the hunters had reached him and pressed a spear to between his shoulder blades.

Knowing he was defeated, Daganu simply relaxed and waited for the killing stroke. This was the fate of animals like himself.

"Who are you?" asked one of his captors.

Daganu tried to speak but it had been many days since he had last shared words with others, and these were not the best of conditions.

He cleared his throat and tried again.

"Say again?"

The speaker looked to his companions. *"Did that sound like good talking to you?"*

"It was close."

"Make him try again."

The first speaker, who was Mackesh, leaned on his spear and studied his captive. Speaking more slowly he repeated, *"Who are you?"*

Daganu felt the first rays of hope. By concentrating he thought he could glean meaning from the others' words. He also spoke slowly.

"I am Daganu of the Kakass."

Mackesh mouthed the words to study them and understand them better.

"Kakass?"

Daganu shook his head to affirm it. "Kakass."

"Where...Kakass?"

Daganu raised his arm slowly, not wanting to startle the holders of so many spears.

"That way, many days."

The actual conversation was more disjointed than this. There were stops and repetitions. Both speakers thought the other had a heavy accent. Rather, they would have thought that if either spoke a language containing that word.

Mackesh made a gesture encompassing himself and all of his companions. ***"Sabba,"*** he said.

He reached with his spear to nearly touch Daganu's injured foot.

"How?"

"Run from Live In The Ground."

Mackesh's face instantly screwed up in distaste. Without speaking he shifted his position and held a hand out for Daganu. After a minor hesitation Daganu took it. Mackesh helped him to his feet.

Speaking to his companions in a matter of fact manner and at normal speed he said, ***"Any person who gets away from those Live In The Ground heretics deserves another chance."***

Once on his feet a thought occurred to Daganu. He hobbled over to the two marmots he still had, lifted them with one hand and offered them to the hunters. It wasn't much but it was literally all he had.

Mackesh realized this and came to an instant decision.

"Ballapak, make a fire. We're going to have a feast." He looked at the rodents and added, ***"A very small feast."***

There are very few rituals which can be found that are part of the culture of every clan throughout the ages. Eating together is one such ritual. The sharing of food has a significance that stretches deep into the past and includes all groups of humans that exist, or that have existed. If strangers eat a meal with each other, there is at least a temporary peace between them.

Everybody recognized the humour in the situation. Although no one got much, everyone had a few tidbits. There was much pantomime of being too stuffed to manage another bite, which was accompanied by laughter.

It was a much more relaxed group of people who rose to their feet. The power of a shared meal was proven yet again. Before Daganu joined them he carefully checked the fire to be certain there were no live coals left. Mackesh watched him but made no comment.

Then they began the long journey back to the Sabba encampment.

With Daganu's injured foot they were unable to move briskly. A runner was sent ahead to tell the Sabba. Some mountain sheep were spotted and hunted. The group managed to bring one down, which was very good news because they were completely out of food. However, it did cost them most of one day.

This interlude served to help build a feeling of comradeship because it was Daganu who first saw the sheep. For his part Daganu felt that by doing this he was able to be something more than a burden. Being a burden is a feeling which is never pleasant.

The young hunter Sutt, who had been the hunter first sent back to the encampment, had been ranging out from that encampment to try to get the earliest alert that the group was near. It was therefore not a surprise that Sutt was the first to see the group approaching. After catching sight of the group and confirming that they were, indeed, the returning hunters, he dashed back to the camp in a quite undignified rush. He didn't care.

The council were gathered and waiting when the expedition arrived. There were fish freshly cooked to greet them. Sutt had been diligent in performing his duties as a hunter. Whether on the land or in the water, prey is still prey, and the pursuit of prey is still hunting.

For all the Sabba hunters there was a great joy in rejoining their clan. They had been gone far longer than expected. Such delays cause real anxiety; they sometimes indicate a serious injury or even a death.

Daganu observed the welcome with some pleasure but it also triggered a yawning emptiness within him. It was as if there was an empty socket where a tooth used to be, but that socket was spread across his spirit. The excited chatter was much too fast for Daganu to follow. He caught the occasional word, but mostly it was only noise.

He did see Mackesh gesturing towards the direction by which he had come. Whether he was talking about Daganu, the Kakass or the Live In The Grounds was not clear to him. He stood waiting for some indication of his fate. He took a little comfort from the fact that they had let him keep his spears. At least they trusted him to not attack an entire clan alone.

Faint praise.

Eventually the elder woman to whom Mackesh had been speaking to left the hunt leader and came over to the unfamiliar young hunter.

"Chief," Daganu said, making a gesture of respect. She acknowledged this.

"Mackesh say I talk slow you understand."

"Most," agreed Daganu.

She studied his face, especially his eyes. She looked down at his foot. *"Hurt,"* she said.

"Toe break. Gets better."

After studying his face for a time, she straightened. Evidently, she had made some decision.

"Wait," she said.

He watched her return to the main group. She gathered some of the elder clanspeople, spoke briefly, and they moved to a location nearby.

After they had settled themselves she gestured to Mackesh. He then walked to where Daganu stood.

"Come," Mackesh said. They walked over to the group of elders who were sitting in a ring

Daganu paused. "What?" he asked, looking to confirm his reading or the situation.

"Council," Mackesh said.

Daganu stopped. He set his gear on the ground. Beside it he placed his spears. Looking at Mackesh he said, "Now."

Mackesh looked at Daganu, then at what he had put on the ground, and back at Daganu. He gestured approval. Mackesh took him to a place in the circle opposite the chief. Daganu noticed that there was no council fire. He thought that was curious. At a gesture Daganu sat. His guide turned to leave.

"Mackesh," the chief said.

Mackesh paused.

"Sit."

After taking a deep breath Mackesh complied. The chief turned her attention to Daganu.

"Now," she said. *"Tell."*

TEN

---

aganu looked toward the distant peaks as the tension settled on him like a stack of skins.

"I..."

He tried again.

"There was..."

He swallowed and fought a wave of sorrow and despair; he was determined to speak his story, even though it hurt.

"In the night, ground shook. Then biggest roar I ever hear...I afraid.

I hunt alone. I don't understand. I need help.

I go to my people; find what happen.

My people not there.

The camp not there.

Side of the mountain not there.

I have no people.

Mountain ate people.

Without people, I nobody. I nothing.

I look for someone. Anyone.

I find Kakass Vag. No good. They beat me. They drive me away.

I find Live In The Ground. No good. They try kill me. I run. I run in river. Leave no sign.

Foot find stone in water. No good. Toe break.

I go high. Is good. Live In The Ground not follow.

I stay high. I have no place to go. I have no people.

Is no good. When winter come, I die."

Daganu sighed in resignation.

"Is all."

It was silent for a while.

"Mackesh," said the chief. *"Tell me your opinion."*

Mackesh quickly organized his thoughts.

"We found his trail in the meadow where Urklan killed the bear.

Ballapak saw it. That was well done because he leaves a very faint trail.

We tracked him from meadow to meadow. It took several days to catch up to him. He did not offer to fight, but instead offered to share what food he had. We let him keep his spears. He did not make us regret this.

As we travelled, he always made sure to leave no sparks in the fires we had made. He shows care for the hunting ground of others. He is quick to notice and to understand.

I would respect his opinion. I would not fear to have him protect my back."

The chief frowned as she considered all that had been said. She motioned both of them away.

Daganu and Mackesh walked a small distance to give the council space to discuss and decide what to do.

They sat quietly for a time. Unusually for this time of the year, a bird was singing nearby; it helped Daganu to relax slightly.

He was reminded yet again that he really liked birds. Somehow things never seemed hopeless when a bird was singing.

Then Daganu said, "They prepare you to be elder."

Mackesh wrinkled his nose in distaste. ***"Don't want. Too much burden."***

Daganu plucked a grass stalk and began to chew on the end. "Not your choice."

"Should be."

"Should, is, different."

They were quiet for a while.

Then Mackesh gestured to Daganu's neck. ***"Teeth. How?"***

Daganu grinned. "You no tell."

"I no tell."

And thus, it happened that Daganu told his new friend the truth. It took a long time as they both struggled with language. Daganu told about mammoths and longtooth cats, and how the mighty killer of the longtooth was a full herd of mammoths, and his role was merely that of a scavenger. Finishing, he thumped his chest and said, "Mighty warrior," and laughed.

Mackesh laughed with him. He gestured to the other hunters. ***"They will tell what they think happen. Much better story."***

"So, they be wrong. They allowed to be wrong. I no argue."

"You will be legend. People tell long time." Mackesh paused, and added, "I no envy."

"Is heavy burden." Daganu put on a martyred expression. "I carry it."

Chuckling, they found more comfortable positions and settled down to wait.

It was a long wait.

As they sat quietly Daganu listened to the birds that were active nearby. He smiled faintly.

Mackesh looked at him quizzically.

"I listen to birds," Daganu explained. "I like birds. Make me happy."

This explanation made sense to Mackesh. He shook his head in agreement. No words were required.

They saw the elders in deep discussion. In time the discussion did end and they began to rise and wander away in different directions. Not terribly long after that they began to assemble at the fire. Sutt came over to fetch them. He sat Mackesh in one place and placed Daganu in another.

The two of them exchanged apprehensive glances.

The chief gestured for silence and the background hum of quiet conversation tailed off into silence. Then, the chief began to speak.

"Daganu of the Kakass, we of the Sabba have sat in council. We have discussed you. We have discussed

the tale you have told. We have discussed what to do about you."

The chief was speaking more quickly and in a more normal tone than when she had addressed him earlier. Daganu could not follow all that was said, but he recognized that she was being formal. This council was going to determine his future, and he had no idea what would come next. He was anxious, tense, and in all honesty, afraid. When he looked across to Mackesh he saw that Mackesh seemed as apprehensive as himself.

"You identify yourself as Daganu of the Kakass, but we say that is not true. The Kakass were eaten by the mountain. They are gone. There is no Kakass. You cannot be part of something that does not exist."

Daganu felt the words in the pit of his stomach, as if he had been brutally kicked. It was nothing he had not thought of himself, but hearing it spoken aloud still hit like a blow from a club. As the Kakass Vag healer had said, that was the magic of words.

And so, he at first missed what the chief said next.

"It is not good that you live without a people. Without a people you live but are not really alive.

Mackesh speaks for you. Mackesh says you try hard to be of value to those who travel with you. Mackesh trusts you. The council trusts Mackesh.

We therefore adopt you into the Sabba. Welcome to the clan."

He was bewildered when a roar erupted from the rest of the clan. Suddenly he was surrounded by a tight mass of humanity. It seemed that every member of the clan wanted to touch him at the same time. He could not make out much of what was said, but over and over one word was repeated: welcome!

He was not alone.

He was welcome.

He was not clanless.

He was human.

And Daganu smiled.